# BEST OF BEST
# GAY EROTICA
# 3

T0056749

# BEST OF BEST
# GAY EROTICA
# 3

*Edited by*

## RICHARD LABONTÉ

CLEIS
PRESS

Published in the United States by Cleis Press Inc., 2246 Sixth St., Berkeley, California 94710.

Printed in the United States.
Cover design: Scott Idleman
Cover photograph: Uwe Krejci/Corbis
Text design: Frank Wiedemann
Cleis logo art: Juana Alicia
First Edition.
10 9 8 7 6 5 4 3 2 1

ISBN: 978-1-57344-410-1

*For Asa*
*...the best is now*

# CONTENTS

# INTRODUCTION:
## VARIETY IS INDEED THE SPICE

Erotica is subjective. What tweaks my nipples might not tickle your libido; what hot-throbs you could leave me cool—and soft. That's both the challenge and the charm of assembling the annual *Best Gay Erotica* anthologies (BRINGING YOU THE BEST IN LITEROTICA SINCE 1996!): transcending stereotypes with lyrical writing, trumping clichés with solid plotting, accepting that variety is indeed the spice of an erotic life. You might find one hot jock, but you won't find a book full of them; here a hustler, there a skater boy, here a Daddy, there a bear cub, here a trucker, there a fratboy, here muscle worship, there twink appreciation, here a whipping, there a fucking, here an anonymous tryst, there two lusty men in love…that range of turn-ons is what sets *BGE* apart from themed anthologies—as does the fact that more than just my sensibility decides each table of contents.

How is that? *BGE* is a judged collection: I select about three dozen stories every year from several hundred that are submitted or that I read elsewhere, but the "bests" are filtered, after my choices, through the literary (and, I assume, lascivious) taste of others.

So when it came time to assemble the third *Best of Best Gay Erotica*, culled from stories published in the 2006, 2007, 2008, 2009, and 2010 collections, I polled each judge for a few favorites from his year.

In his introduction to *BGE 2010*, Blair Mastbaum wrote: "This book is art, really. Sometimes, the sex is secondary. It's the words that are primary." For reprint here, he selected "The Boy in the Middle," by Thom Wolf. "What can I say? English schoolboys do it for me, and Thom writes about sex like I like it—without any special tone to signify the erotic." And he picked "The Stray," by David May. "It's just so great that you don't know if Bud is a dog or a boy or what at the beginning, and the word 'stray' in general is very sexy. Also, I think the rainy, cloudy weather of the Northwest is a great setting for any story."

Blair also singled out "A Beautiful Face," by Robert Patrick: "I like any story with a Greyhound bus in it, and I love the repression depicted of the 1950s" —but you'll have to buy *Best Gay Erotica 2010* to read his third selection, because...

...James Lear (*BGE 2009*) selected "Mass Ass," also by Robert Patrick. His take: "It's sexy, of course, but it also captures all the other crazy things that go through a man's mind when he's having (or hoping for) sex—literary allusions, jokes, puns, et cetera. And, as erotic narrative verse, it's almost unique." In 2009, he summed up his approach to judging erotica this way: "All the stories I have selected...are rooted in reality. They all recognize and respect the fact that sex is most exciting when it arises from the everyday."

Emanuel Xavier (*BGE 2008*) focused in his introduction on how "even the most provocative erotica...reveals the need to connect on a deeper level" beyond the merely physical. For this volume, he selected "Rushing Tide of Sanity," by Charlie Vázquez: "Proving that pain and piss-party perversion can be both profound and pleasurable"; "Orange," by Lee Houck: "A refreshingly twisted sexual experience featuring provocative characters"; and "Underground Operator," by Andrew McCarthy: "This story genuinely captures the wet dreams and raw sexual spirit of Gotham's underground."

Timothy J. Lambert (*BGE 2007*), best known as the coauthor of a number of smart gay romances in which scenes "fade to black" before the sex, said the judging experience motivated him—a self-described recluse—"to get out of my house and look for adventure" of the sorts recounted in the collection. His *Best of Best* picks: "I really liked Alana Noël Voth's 'Benediction,' because it reminded me of classic erotica; there was literary merit as well as an 'I shouldn't be getting off on this, but I am' element within the story. And Drub's drawings, based on Dale Lazarov's powerfully wordless plot! 'The Welcome Back Fuck,' I love that. Totally satisfies the voyeur within to see these two hot drawn dudes be so passionate."

And for Mattilda Bernstein Sycamore (*BGE 2006*), it's all about the reader: "This book is dangerous and lovely, just like you." His picks and pithy summations: "Fucking Doseone," by Ralowe Trinitrotoluene Ampu: "Everything you want is everything you hate and everything you hate is everything you want and this may cause problems"; "The Pancake Circus," by Trebor Healey: "You'll never think about pancakes the same way again"; and "They Can't Stop Us," by Tim Doody: "Sirens call from the distance, but you were made for this city."

I had my favorites, too, more than I could shoehorn into *Best of Best Gay Erotica 3*: the only editing task harder than cramming thirty-five or so fine stories into each year's anthology of fifteen to twenty selections was choosing the fifteen for this collection from ninety-one possibilities. But stories by Steven Zeeland, Shane Allison, Arden Hill and Simon Sheppard stood out for me—Zeeland's for the intensity of his autobiographical experiences, Allison's for its hallucinatory style, Hill's for its intimacy, and Sheppard's for its stylish take on the life of...a writer of erotica.

If you're a regular reader of the *Best Gay Erotica* series, this collection will reconnect you to companionable—dare I say hot?—reads from years past; if you're new to the series, consider this an introduction to a tremendous erotic backlist.

Richard Labonté
Bowen Island, British Columbia

# A RETIRED WRITER IN THE SUN

Simon Sheppard

"Narrative coherence," said the Witch of Capri. "They all want fucking narrative coherence."

Quilty scribbled furiously. He would have brought his laptop to take notes, but he'd been warned beforehand that computers were banned within the sacred precincts of the Witch's cliff-top home. Not even a voice recorder passed muster. Perhaps it was some kind of obscure test, the Labors of Hercules for interviewers. Or maybe it was just the sadism of an old queen.

"And if there's one thing, my son, that life teaches one, it's that narrative coherence—hell, coherence of any sort—is largely an illusion, the fretful workings of a mind struggling to superimpose order on this squalid mess we call life."

That was a nice turn of phrase: "squalid mess." Quilty struggled to get it all down.

"So you would say that you didn't abandon erotic writing, that it abandoned you?"

"A neat formulation, but no. I simply realized that I could

write porn till the crack of doom, and I'd still never succeed in getting it right."

"Getting what right? Never succeed? But..." The Witch of Capri was, after all, perhaps the preeminent voice in the entire history of gay erotica. Under a variety of pen names—some brutish, like "Ramm Hardin," others, like "Firbank Fiore," exuding more than a whiff of camp—he had churned out a remarkable seventy books, more or less, meanwhile maintaining a parallel, highly acclaimed career in Genuine Literature. All that was, of course, why Quilty was there to interview him.

"The ineffability of desire, my lad. Let me tell you a story." The Witch of Capri had, in fact, told a surfeit of stories over the preceding day and a half, but Quilty let him continue. His doctoral thesis, like it or not, depended on the garrulousness of an old man.

"Several years ago, I met this young man—and I mean young, he was nineteen at the time, or so he said—on the phone sex lines." The renowned Witch of Capri jacking off to phone sex? Now *that* was an image. "He was, he told me, tall, skinny, and a redhead, still living with his parents. And he had the softest, shyest, horniest voice. The first time we spoke, he came so quickly that I hadn't time to unzip myself. Subsequently, he'd phone me at odd times when his family was gone, and every time I heard his voice on the phone, I became instantly erect.

"He, for his part, became rather adept at phone sex. He would tell me what he was, or wasn't, wearing, and follow my lead, or at least say he was doing so. I would command him to get some spit on his hand and slide a finger up his ass, and in short order, he'd be making the most delightful moans. He didn't come as quickly as he had at first, either, though he still outpaced me every time. And he did have an annoying habit of hanging up as soon as he'd come, though a 'Good-bye' or 'Thank you' certainly wouldn't have been out of place.

"But that's not really the point, is it? If the redheaded boy had been a character in a story I was writing, I would have been expected to add some narrative aspect, some conclusion, some—no pun intended—climax. His parents would have walked in on him while he had his young dick in his hand. We would have arranged to meet, and would have had fabulous sex. Or he would have turned out to be fifty, bald, and fat. Or something. But none of that happened. He phoned me perhaps a dozen times, got off, hung up, and eventually ceased calling. That was all."

He sipped his gin and tonic and looked off to the horizon, where an improbably lovely sunset, freighted with metaphor, colored the late afternoon. "But the truth is that, more than a decade later, that unseen redheaded boy remains one of my erotic touchstones. After god-knows-how-many tricks in my life—I was quite a looker in my youth, but you already know that—I still desire that voice on the phone more than I've ever wanted just about anyone. And thinking about it still gets me hard." Quilty, unable to restrain himself, looked down. Sure enough, the Witch's rather awful caftan was tenting up.

The Witch of Capri finished off his G&T. "And nothing I could possibly write...well, let's just say that I retired for good reason. Shall we go in for dinner?" He rose shamelessly and, preceded by his famous erection, left the terrace.

The von Gloedenesque serving boy—he reeked of Mediterranean rough trade, and Quilty could only hope he was of age—cleared away dishes that had been licked clean of *panna cotta*, and poured fussy little glasses of port.

"I came, as you're aware, from a good deal of money, so I've been able to afford all this." With a grand sweep of his arm, the Witch indicated his surroundings, including the handsome young man. "And, really, at this stage of my life, there are only two major causes for discomfort. First, there's the inexorable passage of time, which is, you know, or at least can surmise, a bitch. And, perhaps more acutely, there's my utter inadequacy when confronted by the beauty of men...well, let's be honest, *young* men. Of course, I can easily afford to hire company. The financial aspect of such transactions might well be viewed as somehow demeaning, it's true. But when a smooth, slim twenty-year-old strips down, lies back, his lovely cock standing straight up against a jet black thicket of pubic hair, and, at my command, opens his ass to me till I can see the pink corona, glimpse the darkness within..." He sipped the port and stared into middle space.

At last Quilty, concerned the rest of the evening might be a waste, coughed gently. The Witch was brought back. "You know," he continued, "I'd bet that many of us who write dirty stories do it, at least in part, in an attempt to master lust. Not to overcome it, but to make it, through thought and word, our servant. To capture desire, quintessential desire. And in this we are damn well bound to lose.

"Ah, but what's a poor old fag with a penchant for words to do? Become a writer like all the rest, it seems. I knew them all, of course. Tennessee, Truman, Bill Burroughs. They were not happy people. Understatement."

Quilty had been imagining the Witch staring quizzically at some young hustler with his finger up his butt. Now he was afraid that the interview had slid to an end. He had more than enough material, most likely, to use for the thesis, but...

"It all just makes me sad," the Witch concluded. "Melancholy. Sad."

Long, silent moments passed. At last, Quilty spoke up. "Thank you, sir. Thank you for your hospitality, and your time, and your...mind."

"Ah, but surely you're not leaving now?" the Witch said. "It's likely too late to take a train to the airport."

And Quilty had, in fact, planned to spend a second night in the Witch's guest room. "No, I just thought that our interviews were at an end."

"Well, I suppose they are. I've already nattered on far too long. Who knew, when I was churning out pulp paperbacks to be read by closeted, masturbating fags, that I would someday be the subject of something called Queer Studies?"

"Well, you're a great writer."

"No."

"Well, a good writer. An important writer."

"That's closer to the mark, I suppose." A wry smile. "You're rather an attractive young man. But you already know that."

Quilty was blindsided by the shift in conversation. But the Witch was right: he *did* know that.

"So you have, no doubt, been expecting I'd come on to you. More port?"

Quilty shook his head.

The Witch turned to the serving boy, who had been hovering in a corner of the whitewashed room. "You can go now," he said, "and shut the door behind you."

Quilty thought of an old, crass bumper sticker: *GAS, GRASS, OR ASS—NOBODY RIDES FOR FREE.* This was apparently a more literate version of the sentiment.

"Well, you know, I'm certainly more interested in my immortal reputation, however risible that notion may be, than in yet one more penis. I'll bid you goodnight."

Quilty didn't surprise himself too often, but at that moment, he did. "It doesn't have to be goodnight," he said. He tried to sound as insinuating as possible.

"I appreciate that. I can even get over my qualms over being a mercy fuck; after all, it's rather late in the game for me to stand upon my pride. But..."

"Narrative coherence, right? This is what I'm expected to do?" Quilty reached down for his crotch. "What some theoretical reader expects." He sounded, to his own surprise, a bit angry. He did not dare bring up, though, the story an assistant professor had told him of fucking Allen Ginsberg. "He was," the assistant prof had said, "getting old, was surely not very attractive, at least not to me. But that didn't matter, not really. Hell, I was having sex with *Allen Ginsberg*."

The Witch of Capri was staring intently at him. "I have no idea," he said, "what you think you're up to. If you suppose that this is what I expected, a quid pro quo for the interview, then you might think again. I'm an egomaniac, yes, but I would so like to think I'm not that sleazy." He paused, as if for dramatic effect. "On the other hand, you are, as I previously made clear, a remarkably handsome young man. Worthy of a story, really, if I were still writing stories."

Quilty hadn't planned on standing up, but he rose. He hadn't planned on getting hard, either, but something about being the object of laserlike desire went straight to his cock. "I want to do this," he said.

"Well, I've come to the conclusion, I'm afraid to say, that sex is the one wild, true thing. Pray don't let me stop you."

Quilty grabbed at his hard cock through his khaki pants. The shape of the engorged shaft was clearly visible. The Witch of Capri shifted in his chair. "Perhaps I should move to a chaise longue for this?"

"Perhaps you should."

"To the terrace, then?"

"It's private enough out there?"

"Relatively."

"And if someone should see us?"

"Fuck them," said the Witch of Capri.

The evening was warm, and, conveniently, the moon was full. From far below came a gentle sound of waves.

"Ah, time," said the Witch of Capri, his caftan hiked up high on one naked thigh. "You don't mind if I reminisce?"

*That's nearly all you've been doing,* Quilty thought. *That and complaining.* Which brought up, perhaps, the question of just why his hand was shoved down the front of his pants, stirring his cock back into full erection.

"The things people do with their dicks for no particular reason," said the Witch, quite as though he could read Quilty's mind. "Or for some reason that they'd rather not face. So are you going to entertain me or not?"

Quilty unbuttoned his trousers, letting them gap open, revealing well-filled, snowy white briefs.

"I remember when I was in school," the Witch said. "There was this Jewish boy, Chaim. He came from a family of refugees. Nice kid, smart. Beautiful boy, with dark, deep eyes and a Semitic nose. And I was so in love with him."

This line of chat wasn't helping Quilty's erection. He tried to focus in on his dick.

"I didn't do anything about it, of course. Different times. And I was too shy, if you can believe that. But after we'd gone off to college, we met up again one summer afternoon. He was wearing shorts—funny, but I can still remember that, even though much of last week escapes me—that showed off his thin, hairy legs."

Quilty had known someone like that, a Jewish boy he'd fucked. He thought of what that had been like, and his dick got harder. His host didn't stop talking, but it was obvious that he'd noticed—something in his eyes, a change in his tone of voice.

"We went for a walk in the countryside, down by a lake. He wordlessly stripped down, never taking his eyes from mine. His naked body was absolutely amazing. Hairy from the waist down, ass too, but otherwise totally smooth except for bushy armpits. Slim, defined torso, generous nipples. His dick was just average, really, but at the time I didn't know that, and as it got hard, it seemed just huge. I wanted to touch it so much, but I was so very afraid. Chaim turned and ran into the water, leaving me there on the shore with a hard-on in my pants. Several minutes later, after splashing around in the water—which, if I were writing a story, I'd probably describe as 'sun-dappled'—he came out, his dick soft now, and walked right over to me. Without hesitation, I got down on my knees. His was the first cock I ever sucked."

Quilty had stepped out of his sandals and let his pants fall to his ankles. He was rubbing himself through the thin cotton of his briefs. The Witch hiked up his caftan, raising it to his waist. He was naked underneath. Quilty gasped. The man's hard dick was absolutely huge, almost freakishly so.

"Take off your shirt for me," the Witch of Capri asked. Ordered?

Quilty unbuttoned his shirt and pulled it off.

"Very nice. Oh, and lose the pants, too. But keep your briefs on for a while. I like that. I should write about you and your briefs. Who knows, maybe I will."

Quilty knew that the Witch wasn't writing erotica anymore, but he found it an appealing notion nonetheless. *Immortality,* he thought. *Of a kind.* He turned around and played with his underwear-clad ass, then bent all the way over, hoping that the

Witch could see the outline of his balls between his legs.

"Ah," said the Witch, "and such are the consolations of age."

Quilty couldn't decide whether he found that pretentiously self-pitying or not. He stood up straight and said, over his shoulder, "And of fame."

"And fame," the Witch agreed. Was that melancholy in his voice?

Quilty turned to face him. The older man was rubbing his fingertips gently over the underside of his gigantic cock.

"And did you see him again? Chaim?"

"That was a long time ago. Who knows, perhaps the whole story didn't even happen. I am a writer, you know. Many things that should be true, aren't." He looked directly at Quilty's crotch. "Would you like help with that?"

Quilty didn't know what to say. It would compromise his scholarly objectivity—not that that wasn't long since blown away. And being sucked off by a famous pornographer would be something of an experience. At last, he nodded.

"Paolo!" the Witch of Capri called out, and, prompt as a literary device, the serving boy appeared. For Quilty, that was both a disappointment and a relief.

The dark boy, wearing only flimsy white drawstring pants, stood expectantly, waiting to be given his instructions. The Witch snapped his fingers and gestured toward Quilty.

Paolo walked over, stood directly in front of Quilty, and started stroking Quilty's chest, gradually working his way down to his crotch. When Quilty didn't object, Paolo knelt and began to peel down the front of Quilty's briefs.

"I think that you'll find Paolo to be a rather excellent cock-sucker," the Witch said, his fingers still trailing over his dick. "Perhaps the two of you can turn so I can see you better? A profile? Ah, that's it."

"Can I ask Paolo to strip?"

"Of course, my boy. Perhaps you'd like to suck him, as well? I'd enjoy that, I assure you."

At Quilty's terse instruction, the serving boy stood. His white pants were tented out at the crotch. He removed them to reveal a smaller-than-average uncut dick, fully hard. Quilty had him move till the two of them were just a couple of feet away from the Witch of Capri. A sudden, chilling breeze blew up. Quilty dropped to his knees and took Paolo's cock in his mouth.

"You see, Quilty," the Witch said, "there are a number of reasons I decided to conclude my erotica-writing career. But— to make a damaging confession—the major reason, really, was that I concluded that nothing I could write, no matter how accomplished, could possibly capture the beauty, yes beauty, of moments like this."

Quilty felt unaccountably proud. He took all of the small, hard dick deep into his mouth, grabbing Paolo's firm, hairy ass, pushing the cock even farther down his throat. He moved his fingers down the boy's hairy cleft, finding the heat of the slightly moist, responsive hole. The boy began to moan.

"We're trapped in our bodies, you see," the Witch continued, "and sex represents both resigned confirmation of that fact, and an attempt at liberation."

Quilty's pride turned to irritation. *Would you please shut up, you pretentious wanker*, he thought, *so I can concentrate on sucking cock?* He released Paolo's dick, reared back a bit, and looked over to the Witch of Capri. The elderly author, not now touching himself, was sitting there with, astonishingly, tears running down his cheeks. This was all, pretty clearly, more than Quilty had planned on letting himself in for.

He took his hand from Paolo's hole, got some spit on his forefinger. Going back to sucking Paolo's hard dick, he slid his finger inside the boy's ass. Paolo's muscles responded instantly, relaxing so he could get all the way inside the soft, hot hole.

"I've had sex with at least a thousand men," said the Witch of Capri, apropos of nothing. "There's nothing wrong with being greedy, is there?"

*Sex is,* Quilty thought later, on the plane back home, *most always a* de facto *narrative. Beginning, middle, end. Hard to get around that.*

If he had been a porn writer, as the Witch had been, he might have scripted the remainder of the incident with Paolo in one of several ways.

Paolo might, fairly obviously, have turned out to be a hungry bottom, one who got fucked in the evening breeze while his employer watched, jacking off. Quilty would have come inside the boy—sans condom, if he were being daring—and then all three would have buttoned up, perhaps with a bitchy/wise closing remark from the Witch of Capri.

In a slightly more wry vein, boyish Paolo would, lacking self-control, have had a premature orgasm, shooting gob after unexpected gob of sperm down Quilty's gullet. In that case, chances are that both Quilty and the Witch would have been unsatisfied, leaving them with blue-balls-level horny frustration and all its attendant charms.

If things had taken a melodramatic turn, the Witch might have maundered into a full-fledged crying jag. Paolo, the ever-faithful servant, would have fed the elderly author the pacifier that was his penis, and perhaps both he and Quilty would have shot their loads messily onto the Witch's ghastly caftan.

There was a wealth of other possibilities, other turnings. Paolo might, for instance, have turned out to be murderous rough trade, leaving both Quilty and the Witch of Capri sprawled lifelessly in darker-than-night pools of their own blood…though that rather obviously had not been the case.

Who knows? If metafiction were the game, then Quilty might have had no corporeal existence at all, being, rather, an invention of the Witch's still-fertile imagination.

The way things happen, Quilty saw, becomes clear only in retrospect.

Be all that as it may, the morning after *l'affaire Paolo*, Quilty had packed his notebooks into his overnight bag and made his exit. At the door, he hadn't been sure whether to shake the Witch's hand or to give him a hug. But the decision had been made for him. At the very last, the Witch of Capri had embraced him and kissed him on the lips, with an unexpected flourish of tongue. The moment lingered long enough for Quilty to perceive the swelling of the older man's cock, but no longer.

"Just remember to say, Quilty, to quote me to the effect that the current state of erotic writing is lamentable. Lamentable." And the Witch of Capri closed the door.

# RUSHING TIDE OF SANITY

Charlie Vázquez

**Manhattan: Winter, 2007**

I lip-locked with a British punk stud in an East Village dive while Kirsty MacColl warned of chasing bad boys over the shitty speakers—she and I, apparently, both helpless in our ways. Shane's sweat was a magnetic force that drew my lips to his neck, mouth and the bristle around his ears. His heaving core (like an alien about to burst out of his chest) and my long lapses between inhalations of dank air fused together like a courtship ritual dance of manic flightless birds. We left and resumed our noisy *pas de deux* in the cab's backseat.

At his hotel, I initiated the first of many prickly kisses to follow; he hadn't shaved in a couple of days. He let me lead the dance, which I was used to doing anyway. I opened the two buttons holding his shirt up and it fell to the floor like a lopsided theater curtain; a crimson screen of animated tattoos came to life on the stage of his torso when the flickering red lights of the hotel across the street splashed their net of light across us. He kicked his shirt out of the way with his dirty boot and surprised me when he pulled me to him by my wrists, chest to chest.

Our mouths wrestled for dominion, neither of us willing to back down. I rested my hands on the top of his head when I gave in—melting had never felt better. That's how I remember surrendering—I melted into him. It's what I needed and I knew it—I was usually the boss. But not this time. No way. The sweaty bristle on his head was all the aphrodisiac I needed. This was the kind of man I idealized: a cocksucking warrior, a man-fucking descendant of Northern European barbarians who had his image burned into my crosshairs.

Shane shoved me against the wall and tore off my grimy T-shirt, the loud ripping signaling a bone-deep sense of awe and danger. He threw the useless cloth behind him, pulled me away from the wall, and pushed me backward onto the couch. Metal jangled. Magician's hands. He handcuffed my wrists over my head, the cold metal stinging. It was done before I realized it, and the unexpected switch was an extraordinary delight: every aggressor has a unique style, and I would soon catch a fantastic glimpse of his. Little did I know I would stew in it.

As he bit me—*¡Maldita sea la madre!*—I was instructed to address my "boss" as Master Hawk. His advance was swift. The torture of his rough sucking and the scraping of his teeth on my skin sent me into soul-stirring distress. I writhed in equal parts misery and euphoria. The process of surrender began. Wave after wave of ancient music emanated from our cores and through our mouths: the tones of his slick and deep sucking—the ebbing. My guttural heaving for relief—the flowing. In tandem, we were in complete and complex bliss.

I was forbidden to cum.

He fitted me with a restrictive locked cock-cage. *Master*

*Hawk locked my cock away from my hands and the rest of the world!* I started to beg for release, stopped. He uncuffed me and told me to dress. When I was done he cuffed my wrists behind my back. Master Hawk then stripped off his jeans, revealing even more of the inky mosaics of his tattoos—and his sexual fury, which strained up, a veiny reverential salute. He pulled a black NYPD police uniform from his closet, complete with belt, cap, holstered handgun, and nightstick.

Master Hawk had plans. "Stand," he demanded while tucking in his shirt.

I stood, awkwardly.

"Forward."

I did exactly as he said, not more, not less.

"Again," he said while fastening his belt.

I stepped forward until I was face-to-face with him; I oozed at the sight of him in full dress, suppressed my pantings of desire. He uncuffed me and pressed my hands to his swollen crotch— his zone of unresolved pleasure. He kissed me deeply, then spit a slimy cannonball of snot-tinted saliva through my teeth and into my mouth; it tasted like beer.

"Swallow."

I did.

"About face..." I was again handcuffed, this time blind-folded, and led out the door, down the hallway, into the elevator, through the lobby, and onto the street. We boarded a taxi. The driver, I'm sure, added us to his "freaky work stories" category. Master Hawk barked an address. The driver didn't murmur a word. Neither did the Master. The suspense of barreling down midtown streets and avenues, blindfolded and handcuffed, in the middle of the night, thrilled me.

When we arrived, Master Hawk guided me to a freight elevator and we ascended what seemed like ten floors before stopping with a harrowing jerk. I could smell old wood in the air—even mildew and mold. A second voice greeted him; they kissed, I surmised during a brief pause; they discussed "the others."

I heard the breathing of a fourth person.

I was instructed to stand against a pole. Master Hawk kissed me roughly, then the man who had greeted him kissed me; their beards were like steel brushes against my face. Cold beer splashed over me, then my ankles were shackled to the wooden post, splinters ripping into my skin. The cuffs were loosened, then my hands were reshackled in front of my crotch. My cock swelled against the painful restriction of its cage. A bag filled with bottles clattered onto a table, then I heard the unmistakable sound of someone writhing in pain.

"Let's let them see," Master Hawk said.

Our blindfolds were lifted. Three of us were bound to the pole in a triangle. A mustached, muscular, heavily tattooed man of Mediterranean mold was to my right; he was dark with thick black body hair. The base of his hard cock was encircled by a leather-studded cock ring. He sneered.

To my left was a towering black man, hairless, muscled and soaking wet; he too had been splashed with beer, or he was sweating. He had short bleached hair and jailhouse-tattooed biceps scribbled with reapers, tombstones and gang script. He regarded me blankly.

The three of us would be forced to work as a team, in order to serve our bosses. Secretly (or maybe not), we were better off bound the way we were. We would have caused each other untold harm—in order to more selfishly please our masters. That is how determined we were, it was in our eyes.

After taking in the physiques and demeanors of my slave peers, I turned my gaze to Master Hawk's companion. I was taken aback. The second master was a rural warrior from Appalachia or the deserts of Oregon or even Australia's outback. He wore a light gray shirt with EARL written in cursive red script over his left pec. The shirt's armpits were soaked with sweat and his dark blue slacks were marred with grease, a formidable erection evident against the classic worker's fabric. "Earl" was barrel-chested with slicked-back, salt-and-pepper brown hair, a tail of curls dropping from the nape of his neck, with two days of torturous stubble—little spears of gray piranha teeth—on his fierce face.

We were told to call him Baron Trash.

Master Hawk's eyes met mine when I finished taking in the scenario. He approached, forced me to stand tall, then bound me to ceiling restraints, turned to face the pole. He dragged my blindfold back into place and kissed me roughly, from the back of my neck to the cheeks of my ass, his serpent tongue darting in and out, before biting into my armpits, savoring them deeply. Then he drew back from his consumption of me, and the thick tips of his leather flogger tickled my face.

The whip was like an oscillating weapon. Its feather-like tips were as soft as cilia on first contact, but soon accelerated to a force that battered my upper back and then my ass like a boxer's rolling, pounding fist, faster and stronger, next landing with a hissing crash on my left shoulder. I tried to kneel to my left, but was restrained by my bindings.

Something within me collapsed and I allowed myself to fall with it. The skull-rattling blows transitioned to thinner strands that tore at my skin more greedily—cat's claws dragging through skin, razor tips carving designs into flesh. Master Hawk had replaced his original whip with another, one that lashed at my back in horizontal swipes, biting stings from the left and hungry slices from the right. My skin was at once hot and cold. Each strike was preceded by the snakelike hiss of cutting air, which added to the glorious anticipation. My body convulsed. I was more alive with each strike.

Baron Trash unshackled the darkest slave; I heard him crawl forward, heard him slurp on Master Hawk's cock. My Master moaned. I recognized the sound of his breathing and I hated the slave who was sucking my Master's cock, torn by his pleasure at what should be rightfully *mine!*

The sound of Master Hawk's approaching orgasm filled my ears as the full-lipped slave worked his cock like a machine—every wet slurp sounding as though it were happening inches before me. Master Hawk made him stop and struck him in the ass with the nightstick. I was then able to make out the sound of Baron Trash feeling the reward of pleasure seize his fat and dirty dick, as the kneeling slave went to work on him instead. It was apparent that the bare concrete floors stung the slave's knees; his breathing was tinted with a pain he tried to subdue beneath his duty.

The hairy third slave was unbound and forced to suck Master Hawk—I was, by that time, able to tell what was happening by employing the rest of my senses. My jealousy surfaced at the worst of times. I was not allowed to communicate that—though I knew that Master Hawk felt it thickly in the air and was delighted by it. He then instructed the Greek-looking punk slave to lick his balls and boots and accept delicious verbal humiliations, which the Greek slave seemed to derive great pleasure from; his servicing became more enthusiastic with the worsening of the verbal insults.

I was deprived of worshipping the masters at all—I'd been granted a severe punishment. My need for sex became a burning torture in my crotch: I was done with the mind games and was ready to come, but I would need to learn to wait. My deprivation hatched imaginary outcomes in my mind—as to what the rest of the night would lead to.

Our blindfolds were removed again. The black man's mammoth cock was majestically erect. The hairy man's equally massive erection was fleshy and red around the head. My cock was still at bay, incarcerated. We were made to kneel. Master Hawk and Baron Trash set three metal dog bowls down and filled them to overflowing with beer. I knew better than to move. The hairy man did not. He was whipped by the Baron for sipping without first awaiting directions. His bowl of beer was dumped over his head, filled again, put to his mouth, and again dumped over his head, a cruel reenactment of the Curse of Tantalus.

The other slave and I were allowed to drink our beer as a reward. Then all three of us were manhandled into a cage in the center of the room, an enclosure so confining we could only hunch on all fours, side by side, our muscles bunched, our faces strained.

Master Hawk's posture was telling; his shoulders were spread apart, his crotch was pointed forward and his hands rested on his hips, as if examining a situation requiring intervention. The near future was already in his eyes. Baron Trash and Master Hawk unzipped their trousers and showered us with zigzags of warm urine tinted with the unmistakable stench of beer. The chattering cascades of piss were accompanied by their sighs of relief and pleasure, coupled with our very own childish squeals of joy. We were men broken into boys.

When they were done, we were dragged from the cage and the splintered post, piss dripping from our bodies. Master Hawk poured beer over my head—and almost as instantly—licked up the foaming nose-diving cascades. Baron Trash did the same to the black slave and I wondered how the Greek-looking slave felt as Master Hawk made sure to slurp up beer from my armpits, chest, ass and legs. The Greek glared at me.

The cold beer made me shiver.

"Do you have to piss, boy?" Master Hawk asked.

I nodded.

"Then piss."

I was scared—I wasn't sure if I'd been given permission or if I was being tricked. But I lost control of my bladder anyway as another wave of cold beer washed over my head. I shivered uncontrollably as Master Hawk sank to his knees to take in my urinary rush. He held some in his mouth, rose slowly to his feet, and forcefully spat it back in my face.

The feisty Baron then went over to his Greek slave and said, "Hello."

The slave returned the greeting—feeling pressured to speak—and then screamed out for forgiveness when the Baron squeezed the cock ring that encircled his genitals—the kind with studs that dig into sensitive skin.

"You weren't given permission to speak," the Baron growled to the hairy slave.

The slave sank to his knees in a sort of comical Hollywood misery—his face contorting with a severe will not to speak. Our blindfolds were taken away and I wondered what Master Hawk and Baron Trash had planned next. My need for pleasure became a testicular pain, a tension with only one remedy.

What came next relieved my tension. We were to have sex with one another, while my Master and the Baron watched.

The Greek was ordered by the Baron to suck the black slave's enormous curved dick, as the masters masturbated, all the while cruelly critiquing their live sex show. When they'd had enough I was told to eat the Greek's ass while the black slave sucked him. Master Hawk momentarily freed me of the cock-cage—*qué milagro!* This carnal musical chairs went on for what seemed like hours. We were forbidden to come—though we raced closely to it at times, mentally drawing back, communicating through natural sounds of the body that we were flirting with disaster.

When the masters had had enough, I was instructed to kneel before the Baron, the black slave before Master Hawk. The Greek lingered behind us, shivering in a puddle of piss, beer and sweat. We were freed of our handcuffs and told to unzip the masters before us and "finish them off." I happened to look over at the black slave as he put Master Hawk's dick in his greedy mouth. Baron Trash caught a whiff of my jealousy and slapped my cheek to remind me of what I was supposed to be doing.

During the grueling session before my second master, I talked myself out of believing what I thought I was hearing. The masters seemed to be coordinating their arousal. The sound of their approaching orgasms became louder as we synchronized to form a team. We were as two turbines sifting the same current.

Master Hawk then commanded the Greek to put a rubber on and fuck the black slave; I still wasn't sure why I was being left out of so much. The Greek was allowed to come, and he came in a consistent and building bombardment of the black slave's ass—in endless and greedy grunts of relief, he slipped off his target and leapt back onto it, like a crazed dog. The dark slave barely squinted as this happened and continued suckling. The Baron poured more beer on my head, set his bottle down and groaned from a deep place. Master Hawk heaved deeply, spoken language eluding his tongue.

The masters then rushed simultaneously; each leading the other upward in pulsating fits of ancient ecstasy, their loud moaning mounting in length and volume. The Baron anchored his greasy hands onto the back of my head—to make sure my mouth wouldn't separate from his boiling pleasure. The masters came in a duo of operatic beauty—two commanding basses bending to sensitive tenor. They barely relinquished control and gave out orders as soon as their eruptions of passion had passed and dripped from our eager lips.

The Greek had come as well as our masters. The black slave and I hadn't and I was deeply wounded when Master Hawk had me crawl over to him so he could put my cock-cage back on. He tongued me passionately, in wide arcs of dominion. The black slave was told to masturbate. The slicked, gliding motion of his fingers and hand around his remarkable member entranced me.

He locked eyes with me. We communicated visually. Our souls had sex through the intercourse of our uninterrupted stare: I at times staring deeper, he at times surpassing my intensity. I perceived what I believed to be an effort on his part to soften his stance—in order for him to orgasm. I could feel him retreating from—what seemed like—an occupation of my conscience. I then played my silent role as alpha slave: I had the final word, as far as slaves were concerned, and my sneer, stare and stiffness would show it.

The dark slave then shuddered madly; he fell to his side as explosions seized hold of him—he came repeatedly into a puddle of piss and beer while staring through my eyes at a dimension behind me. Master Hawk and Baron Trash seemed impressed. The three of us were uncuffed and handed our clothes and knapsacks. Master Hawk demanded I wait for him once I was done. It wasn't yet clear if our roles had been terminated for the night or if we were still under their command.

I showered—barely.

The other slaves left without cleaning up at all.

I never found out what happened to Baron Trash.

\* \* \*

Shane and I taxied back to the hotel. Other than being uncomfortable (I still had my crotch-cage on) and feeling *used*, I felt a sudden need to fight—which I was known to do rarely. Once we arrived at the hotel, we ascended many staircases and I demanded to be set free. Shane, shed of his alter ego, was a bit less severe, yet he seemed uninterested in me.

"Arms up," he said.

I lifted my hands to mouth level. Shane unlocked the cuffs and removed them. He then had me sit, in order to remove the cock-cage. My despair surfaced as rage. I wanted to scream for something but he muted my grief with his firm lips planted on mine. He then stepped back, lifted the cuffs to me and said, "I am now *thine*."

I cuffed him over his head, laid him on his belly and savored the reward of all my labor—his hairy ass. I returned his punishment through the hardness and hunger of my profound, almost spiritual, need. All the rage of my ancestors surfaced to feed my desire and the occupation of his ass—ghosts in my head shouted for freedom and drove me forward. My primordial demons feasted in the carnal celebration—they danced through fire—as I scaled the rungs of overload and came—*¡puñeta!*— with his rock-hard, mural-rich biceps in my hands, my nose pressed into the sweaty patch of bristle by his ears. I rolled off of him. My mouth split open as if I'd just died and a tide of sanity rushed over me.

When it passed, Shane asked me, "So what'd you think?"

"That I have the coolest fucking boyfriend in the universe."

Then we slept divinely, entwined like lazy vines.

# BENEDICTION

Alana Noël Voth

I'm naked. I can't see anything; it's dark. I hope I'm in Cheeseman Park. Mom and I used to go there with Mom's friend, Ryan. We'd sit at a picnic table and eat chicken and salad. I remember one time after lunch, I was like seven, I went down the slide on my belly just to get that rush in my gut—that thrill of being, for one second, out of control, rushing headlong at the gravel with my hands out and face forward. Later, I buried my legs in the sand, and then my knees rose from the dead.

I used to look at pictures of men in *GQ* and *Esquire* and wonder what it would take to get a man to love me. I was ten and obsessed with love. Ryan found me gazing at a black-and-white spread of a male model once and said, "Brenner, what are you looking at?"

I pointed at the male model.

"Listen, Brenner. You like guys; that's okay. I want you to know it's okay. Your mom loves you. I love you too. I'm gay. You knew that. Right. So listen, I don't want to scare you, but it can be...complicated. Know what I mean?"

Mom loved me.
Ryan loved me.
I believed someone else would love me too.

Not that I lived in a perfect world. Grand Junction wasn't a gay boy's Utopia. I knew the most insulting thing you could do was call a guy a faggot. By the time I was in kindergarten I knew you could be a leper or a homo, there wasn't much difference. In first grade, I sealed my fate. I told my classmates when I grew up I'd write books and marry a man. I was by myself after that. Always. Teachers expected me to be attentive and get good grades but then looked at me like I had a booger on my finger and was going to wipe it on them.

It's dark. I'm naked and lying on some grass; I must be in Cheeseman Park, because I feel the grass blades like a cool prickly blanket beneath my skin. I used to lie in the backyard with nothing on and enjoy the tickle of grass against my ass and shoulders. A sprinkler would come by and douse me with mist. I lay there and played with my dick. My dick would get hard and even have a feeling like coming, except nothing would come out, no jizz.

I'll imagine my lungs are an accordion—you know, those things that a person plays by pushing it in and then pulling it out and it makes noise like wheezy music.

In and out, in and out, that's good, that's good; keep it going.

I hear an owl hooting and try and hoot back. I've always wanted to do that. I can't. Maybe I gurgled. Is it late? I want to feel the sun on my face. I don't want to be scared. Oh fuck, I'm scared. I miss Ron. Everything hurts: My chest, my throat, my whole body. Feels like I got thrown around in a car. I remember a car going fast. A car accident? They say your life flashes before your eyes. Maybe I should close mine.

I used to close my eyes in Mom's car. She liked driving her convertible Volkswagen Beetle with the top down. Sometimes we'd drive through town—Mom with her blonde hair blowing behind her, and me waving at everyone like they were friends.

On the stereo, Johnny Cash sang: *Love is a burning thing, and it makes a fiery ring, bound by wild desire; I fell into a ring of fire.*

When I was in sixth grade, Ron McDermott and some other guys were in someone's garage playing with matches and gasoline. Something about *they were going to build the biggest most terrifying bonfire any man had ever seen!* Then Ron went up in flames and according to some reports was ruined, destroyed, painful to look at, to see. He spent months in the hospital having skin grafts and physical therapy and still he was badly scarred.

When Ron came back to school, he wore a flesh-colored bodysuit under his clothes and one half of his face was red and swollen. He did look a little lopsided. Mostly he looked sad. Other kids avoided him or stared when they thought he wasn't looking, which made me mad, made me defensive.

But something else.

Part of me, an inside thing, like a spirit or an emotion, *something eternal* reached out to him, wanted to touch Ron, comfort him, and make him smile again. I recognized another tortured soul, I guess, another straggler, black sheep, leper.

I approached him one day on the playground.

"Want to play tetherball or something?"

Ron McDermott looked at me. He wore a hat, I think to keep his scars out of the sun, which made me sorry because I loved the feel of the sun on my face.

"I'm not supposed to," he said. "Moving too much stretches

my scars then they hurt or they might tear, then I'd have to get more grafts and that sucks."

"Oh." I hadn't thought of that. I felt stupid. "I'm really not into tetherball. I mean what's the point?" I laughed, shaking my head, trying to make him feel comfortable, trying to relax. "What about jacks?"

"Jacks?"

"Yeah, with the ball and the jacks…."

Ron raised one eyebrow. He had perfect eyebrows. They hadn't been burned off. He also had beautiful eyes—very green.

"Isn't that like a girl's game?" he said.

I shrugged. "Is it?"

Come to think of it, I'd only played jacks with girls, mostly Jill and Susanne, who didn't drive me crazy saying, "I wish you weren't gay, Brenner," and "What a waste," or "C'mon, Brent, kiss me. See what you think."

Why did I have to do that? So I'd be normal, okay?

Ron smiled. "It's totally a chick game."

I laughed. "Guess so."

After a moment Ron cracked a smile.


We were together after that—a gruesome twosome. Inseparable, coconspirators, buddies. When teachers said our names out loud it was always "Brent and Ron" or "Ron and Brent," but never just one or the other.

One day Ron said, "I'm happy we're friends." Then he punched me in the shoulder.

I rubbed my shoulder then punched him back. "Me too."

To tell the truth, he was my soul mate, my other half.

And you can weather any storm like that. Face any demon.

\* \* \*

We hung out and listened to music. Ryan was constantly giving me old stuff, so Ron and I made mix tapes, odd compilations like "Why Me?" by Planet P followed by "Dreaming" by Blondie, then "Lola" by the Kinks, and then "New Moon on Monday" by Duran Duran, and then "Ballroom Blitz" by Sweet. I'd dance to that one, get goofy bouncing around and shaking and doing the robot, and Ron would sit on the floor near the cassette player and laugh.

I loved his laugh; it was a musical kind of sexy laugh. It egged me on. I'd get goofier just to hear him.

Sometimes Ron would drum a beat on his legs or shake his head so his bangs flopped. He couldn't dance because he still had to watch what he did physically, and his movements were limited, like he couldn't lift his arms too high because the bands of new skin they'd put on him were still tight. He said it felt like wearing a shirt that was too small. He said he felt like a retard because of his physical limitations, because he had to go to therapy with kids who were missing limbs and wore leg braces, and because every morning he had to strip down in front of his mother so she could rub lotion into his scars.

"I feel like an ugly retard," he told me one afternoon. We were in my room on the floor surrounded by tapes.

"You're not ugly." I told him. Not to me he wasn't. I pawed through the cassettes and found something new, the Goo Goo Dolls, and put it into the player.

"C'mon," Ron said. "You see how people look at me—like I'm Frankenstein. No girl is ever going to touch me. All I'm ever going to get is my mom rubbing lotion on me." He put his face in his hands. "No girl is ever going to touch me." He started to sob—a hoarse wretched sound that twisted my gut and broke my heart. "I'll be like that guy in *Mask*," he choked. "He's so ugly his mother has to buy him a hooker."

What did I say? *It's not true. You're not ugly. Forget girls.*

"I'll do it," I said.

"Do what?" Ron lifted his face. Tears and snot glistened across his red scars.

"I'd touch you. I mean, you know, rub lotion on you."

He wiped his nose on his sleeve. "What?"

"I'd do it if you want."

Ron stared at me. "You're just trying to make me feel better."

"No," I said.

We went quiet, listening to the tape.

We had a sleepover once. I stayed the night at his house. We stayed up until three watching MTV then *The Sixth Sense* on video and then getting freaked out by the movie and talking about whether it would be possible to talk to the dead. We also made plans to go to the same college. Ron wanted to become a plastic surgeon and help other kids who were burned. I wanted to be a writer and write love poems.

The next morning, Ron's mother called him downstairs so she could rub lotion on him. He looked at me. I nodded like, okay, go. After a while, I couldn't help it. I wandered from his room down the hallway, down the stairs and then around the house until I found the door to the room open. Spare bedroom, I guessed. Ron lay on a bed. Nothing but a sheet on a mattress.

He was naked on his stomach with his head turned toward the wall, maybe staring at the swirls of paint and seeing pictures—maybe himself not burned. I sucked in my breath. He was nearly skeletal, so thin, and his skin was a twist of stark white and purple, like a candy cane. His mother sat on the edge of the bed and leaned over him, working lotion into his scars: Across his shoulders, down each arm, and then to the slope of his back.

His ass was white and round. I felt the forceful stir of my erection. His mother concentrated on what she was doing, tending her wounded boy. I knew then I wanted to tend him too: I'd do anything. Ron turned his head and saw me. My heart waved. After a moment he barely lifted a hand and wriggled his fingers at me. I nodded then backed out of the door.

It was the summer after eighth grade when Ron told me, "I was so fucking glad when I was conscious enough in that dumb hospital to look down and see my dick was there. It wasn't burned off."

He sighed and looked truly relieved.

"Yeah, I know what you mean."

I began to wonder about Ron's dick. Short and fat; long and curved? Average length? Ethereal? Did hair grow around his balls? What did his balls smell like? Would his come taste like rice pudding?

"There was a nurse that really turned me on there."

"What?" I'd been lost in a daydream.

"A nurse," Ron repeated. "A couple times I beat off in my hospital bed, under the sheets, thinking about her tits."

We were in Ron's room. The window was open. A cool breeze drifted in and tickled my skin. From the cassette player Melissa Etheridge sang, *I'm the only one to walk across a fire for you.*

"Really?" I'd beat off plenty of times thinking about Ron.

"Guess you don't think about chicks," Ron said.

"Umm, no…" I laughed. Dorky nervous laughter.

"What do you think about then?"

Another laugh. "I don't know."

"Is it a particular guy or something?"

"Why?" My heart had begun to beat faster. Maybe he wanted me to say I thought about him when I beat off.

"Tell me," Ron said.

"Okay." But then I didn't say anything.

"C'mon. What's the matter?"

I finally came up with something. "Circle jerks."

"What's a circle jerk?" Ron laughed.

"Guys jerking off in front of each other." I started to laugh again, really nervous. Really hopeful.

"No shit." Ron seemed to think about it. "You ever do it?"

"No."

"Why not?"

"I don't know."

"Never met any guys who wanted to?"

"I guess." I could feel my armpits sweating, my arms shaking, and my dick had started to move. I ran my hand through my hair, trying to think about something else—the rain in Spain, something.

"Want to?" Ron asked.

"What?" Had my voice changed an octave?

"Jerk off."

I looked at him. "You want to jerk off in front of me?"

He was quiet. Then he said, "Well yeah. I mean I'm not queer. We're just friends, and I trust you."

*Maybe he just didn't think he was queer.*

I stared at him until my eyes watered. After a while Ron unzipped but didn't pull his dick out. Mine was already hard. I couldn't see his. Was he hard?

I unzipped. I had a nice dick, average length and all. I wanted Ron to look at it, want it. He looked for a minute then pulled his dick out. It was hard and as sweet as I'd seen in my dreams, average length but thick; his pubes were dark, and his balls looked heavy. I wished I could inhale his balls, lick them. Oh god, I began to jerk off. We jerked in unison. I'd never done this with anyone. I felt exposed and wished we were closer together. If I moved a little...there, our knees touched. I leaned back, pulling on my dick, teasing the head with my thumb. I pressed my knee against his. Ron looked at me.

"Oh god," I said. "Shit." I was going to come.

"Go," he said. "Shoot."

It was almost invisible to the naked eye, the eighth color of the rainbow, actually. Our come in the air together.

"Curtis Winters," I told him one afternoon that same summer. "Peewee baseball. I never saw a guy move like that. Looking at him gave me a stomachache."

Ron nodded. "April Reynolds. Before I got burned. She had long hair and this awesome smile. I wanted to feel her up."

He looked defeated, thinking about April Whoever, thinking about girls. I figured it was my duty to make him feel better since I was secretly madly in love with him. "Lie back," I said.

Ron lay back. I lay next to him, heart beating.

"Close your eyes. I'll close mine."

"Yeah, okay."

"Think of April, what's her name?"

"Reynolds."

"Yeah, think of her."

"Okay."

"What's she doing?" *The bitch.*

"Sitting in the desk across me in Ms. Morgan's class."

"And you're checking her out?"

"Well, yeah. Always."

"Imagine she wants to kiss you." Maybe I didn't sound enthusiastic enough. "She wants to suck your face off." I could smell Ron's hair, his shampoo, the lotion his mother rubbed in his skin. "Imagine soft lips and a warm tongue," I whispered.

Ron turned his head toward me. We were close enough to share breath. When he blinked I could have sworn I felt the soft flap of his eyelashes. I heard when he unzipped his pants, and then he grabbed my head and pulled me toward him.

I hesitated. "You really want to?"

"Do you want to?"

"Yeah."

"I'm not queer," he said, "I just want you to do it."

*God, oh god, at last.* I opened my mouth then my throat and then eased my mouth down his shaft and felt the ridges and veins against my tongue and tasted his salty skin.

I sucked and licked and slobbered.

Ron lifted his hips off the bed, fucking me in the mouth.

I stopped and looked at him. "Ron?" I wiped the saliva off my chin.

He leaned back on his elbows, breathing heavy. Pre-come bubbled on the head of his dick. "What, what is it?"

"I don't know," I said at last. I took hold of his cock again and then pushed my face to his balls and breathed him.

He put his hand on my head. "It's okay," he said.

I hadn't realized I was crying a little.

By high school, you could barely tell Ron had been burned. He had a few scars on his face, more on his back and arms, but they weren't as red or angry looking anymore, not swollen. He stood taller in the hallways and met people's eyes. Once in the lunchroom he slapped some guy a high five. "Who was that?" I asked.

Ron shrugged. "Some guy in my geology class."

"The walls in the john have been newly decorated," I said. "Have you seen it?"

"Nah, I don't think so. What is it?"

"Brent Johnson is a flaming fucking faggot."

Ron shook his head.

"Careful, I might be contagious," I said, nudging him in the side.

He smiled. "Yeah, whatever. Just ignore that shit."

Girls looked at him. I saw them looking at him. They finally saw what I saw. Ron-beautiful-Ron with his thick dark hair and green eyes. His beauty gave me a stomachache sometimes. I'd call him on the phone just to hear his voice. I asked him all the time about college.

One afternoon I said, "What about CU in Boulder?"

Ron looked at me and then said, "Let's get the hell out of here," and I said, "All right," and we walked out of the school building to a lone willow tree that grew past the parking lot. I had him all to myself now and stared at the sky and said, "It's gorgeous."

The willow tree wept branches near a chain-link fence that encircled a field of cattails and wildflowers behind us. Ron shook two cigarettes from a pack of Marlboro Reds. "Here." He offered me one.

I sniffed the end, bittersweet.

Ron held out a lighter, a little unsteady, the flame flickering, and we met eyes over the fire. I wanted to say, "I love you, man." *I love you.* But I inhaled instead, and the butt of my cigarette gave way to ember, and I coughed.

Ron looked away, lighting his smoke. He turned his eyes to the willow then leaned back, his hair falling into his eyes. With one hand, I touched his elbow. He crossed his arms over his chest, didn't say anything, and didn't look at me either.

The sun has come up. But the air feels cold on my skin, biting, because I'm naked and hurt and here alone. It hurts to shiver.

It hurts to think and remember. I can't move voluntarily. Just shiver. I stare through the tree at the sky and then stare at the leaves on the tree and try to focus and wish for the leaves to fall and coat me.

The natural process of breathing is agony. Was he like that, really, Ron groping a girl? When I turn my head, I see my clothes lying on the grass beside me. Ten hours ago, I was driving. I drove Mom's car off an interstate and onto this winding path of asphalt with road signs warning NARROW ROAD and NO PASSING. I had a map beside me, but the map had been handwritten and then photocopied, and things were scratched out and written over. I couldn't exactly read it. I wasn't sure I wanted to go to a party anyway. SENIOR BASH! GRADUATION! I surveyed the road ahead of me and thought how it was the sort of road where if I were trapped in a horror movie, I would happen upon a hitch-hiker with an axe, or someone possessed by a demon speeding up to run me over.

A few miles later, I pulled over and sat at the wheel and took a deep breath. Was I ready to see him? What would I see? These past three months, we hadn't talked much. He had excuses not to get together. I got out of the car and started walking. I stuffed my hands in my pockets. Was he going to break my heart?

A white glow floated ahead and became a sign through the trees. TRESPASSERS WILL GET A FOOT UP YOUR ASS. The red letters were scrawled over white paint peeling away to reveal blond wood. I stopped, looking at it, and thought about turning back, getting in my car, going home. Mom and I could do some-thing—get ice cream, watch a movie, play cards. Big deal, I was graduating high school.

Maybe I should call Ryan and ask for advice. *How to get over a man?* No, better: *How to make him love me.*

The no trespassing sign was hung on a barbed wire fence. I

pulled the wire apart and then stuck one leg through, twisting my body beneath it then through it. I heard music and tracked the thump across the meadow to another border of trees. When I came out past the trees, I stared into the smoky heat from a bonfire and wondered if Ron was right there standing close to the flame?

Jill rushed up and hugged me then gave me a beer. She was with another girl. I didn't see Ron. Jill talked. "We thought we'd stay here awhile then head back to town and go to that bar, remember?"

I nodded.

"You drove, right?"

I nodded again.

"Where's your car?"

I jerked my head toward the orchard.

"You came the back way?"

"Yeah, I guess."

"Jill says they don't card at this bar," the other girl said.

I saw him. Ron with a chick. He had his arm around her. She had one hand in his back pocket, squeezing his ass.

Sometimes, I could still taste his come in my mouth.

Jill nudged me. I pretended to focus on finishing my beer.

"Brent," she said. "Brenner?"

"Think I could get another beer?" I asked.

"Don't go anywhere," she said before heading off.

I headed in Ron's direction. "Hey," I said when I reached him.

Ron smiled and then looked at the girl and said, "This is Brent."

She smiled, a little.

"Can I talk to you?" I asked him, ignoring her.

"Yeah, what about?" He had a blank face, no expression.

"Alone. Over there." I nodded over my shoulder.

The girl snaked her arm around his waist.

"I'm kind of with Connie," he said. "How about later?"

"Well, I kind of need to talk to you now."

The girl glared at me.

"Yeah, okay." Ron walked a few feet away. I followed.

"What are you doing?" I asked him.

Ron looked over my shoulder. "Kind of on a date." He smiled.

I moved close and pushed my face in his neck and held him. "I miss you," I said.

"Ron?" The girl was back.

He pushed me away, but I didn't go too far. "I love you," I said. "Okay? I want you to know that."

The girl stood next to Ron. "What? Are you some kind of faggot?"

Ron looked nervous. "We'll talk some other time, okay?"

I stepped forward again and grabbed him by the head and stared in his eyes and wouldn't let go. "It's me," I said. "Brent."

Ron held me back by the collar. "Stop it, okay? Just stop."

"Let's go," the girl said.

Other people stood around gawking. "Hey McDermott, Connie! You in or not?" Some guys a few yards away were waving to them, waiting. They looked at me, and the look said, *You're not invited.*

For one second, we locked eyes, Ron and me.

"Fuck you," I said.

He leaned over and whispered, "I didn't choose to be a freak, Brent. You did."

I stood there unable to move or speak. The girl wrapped her arms around his shoulders. He disappeared in a smudge of smoke and heat. People walked by, gawking and smiling. I didn't care. I hated them. Then I noticed a guy sitting on the back of a truck by himself. Blond as sunshine, alone. He looked me over then looked away. What the hell? I walked over and stared at him.

"What are you looking at?" he said.

"Nothing."

"Yeah, right."

I could have walked away. He grabbed my arm at the wrist. "Lover's spat?"

"What? Fuck no." I felt mean now, spiteful. There was something dangerous about this guy; I knew it and got a chill but then followed him anyway.

I love it when men kiss. Eye contact first. Then shared breath. Gentle lips. A little tongue. More lips. More tongue. They suck each other's lips. Whirl their tongues around. Moaning. They hold each other's heads. They get rough. Or they're gentle.

I was shoved into a car from behind. Two hands on the back of my head. My forehead hit the roof as I went. Then I was shoved into a seated position on the backseat. The car began moving. Two guys sat on either side of me. Up front, the guy I'd been kissing was driving. Another guy in the front looked over the seat at me.

"What the fuck you looking at?"

I looked away.

They started talking.

"Let's dump him in the faggot park."

"Yeah, the dumb fuck."

I started crying.

The guys in back began slugging me with their fists.

\* \* \*

I had a pet rat once. Daxter. He got sick. His pale-yellow sides heaved as he struggled for breath, and red stuff leaked from his eyeballs. I touched his fur with my fingertip, and he squeaked. I touched him again, and he squeaked. I wanted to hold him, comfort him, except when I touched him, he squeaked. Then he began trying to drag himself away from me. So I wouldn't touch him.

I tried to drag myself away from them. They kept kicking and slugging me. I begged them to leave me alone.

Sunlight. I feel it on my face and imagine a perfect circle around me, like a circle they draw in voodoo to protect or keep evil spirits away. How long will I last? Where am I bleeding? Mom? I see her patching a hole in the knee of my jeans, which is weird, because I haven't worn those jeans since I was ten. I watch her work the needle into the denim, pull the thread out, work the needle into the denim, pull the thread out. *Mom, I can't wear those jeans anymore.* I hear voices. I try to say something. *Over here, the naked beaten boy.*

Someone is above me like a streak of white light before becoming a face. I don't know him. Should I fight? Is it over?

I feel a hand cupping my forehead, a warm touch. "We've got you now," he says. "You're all right. Can you hear me?"

There's this song by Madonna. One of the lines goes *We only hurt the ones we love.* I want to ask this person above me, *Do you think Ron loves me?* But I can't spit the words out, only a little blood.

# THEY CAN'T STOP US

Tom Doody

I'm waiting for the sun to set, for my shift to end, so I can pedal into my favorite part of Manhattan, an emerald oasis right in the center of all the concrete canyons. But I'm so not there yet. On Broadway, I steer my road bike between columns of men (and some women) doing the black-suit-shuffle, cut west to pick up my thirty-fourth package of the day at the World Financial Center, turn east to drop off at 120 Wall Street, and then north to an alley in Chinatown where I climb the stairs to the second floor and hand over a manila envelope to a man who kneads his hands behind a counter. As I wait for his signature, I inhale the incense from a candle-lit Buddhist shrine. Behind him, several rows of women move fabric through the stabbing needles of sewing machines.

I plummet back down the stairs, skipping over every other step, and ponder the sheer number of daily encounters in this city, their anonymity and intimacy, how cultures clash, cavort, merge. Then I'm back in the streets jostling with vendors and taxis and tourists, everybody staking out a claim to space. Sirens scream. New sweat drips down the old sweat that's caked to my face from the last seven hours of exertion and summer heat.

Sometimes, I hate that I get CEOs what they need, when they need it, in death-defying time, for semiadequate wages. Maybe that's why I scream a war cry as I near a crosswalk filled with commuters moving against the light. My voice and my barreling bike part the commuters so fast that one guy's knees jerk up high enough to almost touch the tip of his nose. It takes me ten minutes to stop laughing.

Once I get through Midtown, weaving between cars that stop and go and shift lanes, I drop off my last parcels, radio in to say see you tomorrow. I turn my bike from the four lanes of 59th Street into Central Park, where the noise of the city subsides to a hum. A dozen blocks later, on a footpath, I unhitch the Kryptonite chain from my waist and wrap it around the bike frame and a bench. Finally.

I peel off my sweaty T-shirt, stuff it into the messenger bag that's still slung over my right shoulder, and plop onto the bench to watch the sun crouch down behind the Beresford, the twin-towered San Remo, and the other buildings of the Upper West Side. Then I slink along the dirt paths of the Ramble, around its oaks, maples, and glacial rocks, and stop near a footbridge spanning a brook. The minutes slip by, taking the last bit of natural light with them.

A clear night here turns strangers into silhouettes. But on a cloudy night, like tonight, the eternal lights of New York City are captured and then refracted in an orange glow that peeks under tree tops and reveals glimpses: shiny Adidas pants with racer stripes hugging boy hips; a nipple ring glimmering in the light down of a defined chest; a knit cap above a square jaw.

Two guys stare each other down like gunslingers about to draw. I hear footsteps. I glance behind me, see tousled hair and lips forming a soundless *coo*.

Punks are so hot, the guy I'm looking at says in a voice as serpentine as his fingers sliding through my bleach-blond dreadlocks. His hand doesn't stop at my shoulders, where my hair ends, but meanders around my messenger bag and then traces down my lateral muscles. I suck in summer air, arch my back. He slips his fingers inside my spiked belt and combat pants, snapping the band of the neon yellow spandex shorts beneath.

He leans in closer, till his chest hair tickles my back. I smell sandalwood and sweat. I turn toward him.

Like what you see? he asks.

He steps into a shard of that orange glow: stubbly cheeks, the indent of tight abs above his profiled hips. He's Middle Eastern, maybe Latino. It's too hard to tell out here. He wears jeans and, like me, no shirt.

I nod.

I reach down, feel along the zipper of his jeans. The bulge beneath pushes back. It's never hard for me to get laid out here. I mean, I might gorge on a pint of Ben and Jerry's for breakfast but I burn it off before noon and don't have an ounce of fat on my body, and all the biking has hardened my calves, my thighs, my ass. But still, this guy—Snake Boy, that's what I'll call him on account of his voice and fingers—he's so fucking hot.

We step off the path, back up against the bark of an oak, and I'm rubbing his rounded biceps. They're so slick with sweat that my hands glide. I lean in and exhale heat into his ear and massage it with my tongue. He moans and says, I love your pink nipples. He clenches down on one of them, shakes it around in his teeth.

I unzip his jeans and he tugs down my combat pants, which

land on the ground with a metallic *thunk* 'cause of the spiked belt. His cock bounces out and mine is still sheathed beneath the spandex until he reaches in and swings it around, my cock head brushing against the fabric for two seconds of too much sensation before it's free. And there's that feeling of being naked outdoors, my hips so sensitized to the slight swirl of breeze.

Snake Boy licks my neck, looks up into my eyes, and maybe it's the darkness but his black lashes look like eyeliner.

Here, he says, breathe. He holds a small bottle to my nose. When I inhale, the pungent chemicals burn my nostrils, everything melts, and I'm just a flushed face and a beating heart. And a stiff cock. Which he slides a hand up and down. I'm jerking him off too. With my other hand, I probe the spot right behind his balls. I'm sucking his tongue and the whole world is reduced to me and him. We're pulsing flesh, a single heartbeat.

Suddenly everything turns bright white as if the sun has risen to its zenith. But it's nine o'clock at night. When my eyes flash open, I see that the light emanates from what must be an electric cop car, the kind with a silent engine. I yank my pants up as fast as I can. Too late, way too fucking late. My hands shake. Red and blue lights flash behind the white. Snake Boy grabs my hand and says Run, and he runs and I stumble and then run. Next thing, sirens scream and hard-shelled feet clomp the earth behind us and our hands break apart so we can run faster—through brush, I feel stings, know my calves just got shredded, but it doesn't even hurt; up over this steep knoll and slipping, tumbling down the other side; into more brush, Snake Boy's still right in front of me. We're long-stepping rock to rock along a narrow stream and then running on the other side. We duck down into a gully. Angry voices, radio static, the crunch of foliage. These sounds get louder. And recede. My arteries throb, my chest heaves, and Snake Boy has his hands on his knees as he draws in ragged breaths. We stay crouched for fifteen minutes until he says he knows a place where they won't find us.

A year ago, when I was twenty-five, I first stumbled into the Ramble. Since then, I've made it the finale to my evening commute. The Ramble is a micro-forest in the heart of Central Park. Paths grip cliffsides, double back, and meander along slopes. The dense brush and trees provide an infinite variety of alcoves. At its southernmost point, this cock-shaped peninsula projects into Azalea Pond, a topographical totem to the men who have been coming here for over a century. And still they come: uptown boys in do-rags, downtown artists wearing paint-spattered pants, even middle-aged men from the Upper East Side. Just trees and rocks and sky and us.

And, obviously, cops. They patrol in vehicles or wear plain-clothes to try to surprise us. Queers scatter under the beams of headlights or, after a big bust, line up in handcuffs.

It's not like I wouldn't have run. I just got totally startled. I mean, you should've seen what I did to the cops last month after they fucked with me. I had just walked down the gravel path of the peninsula. At its proverbial head, this cop shined a light in my face.

Did you lose your dog? he asked me.

I saw a poodle around here somewhere, another cop said.

I turned around to leave and they got into their souped-up golf carts and followed me, the headlights blazing on my back-side. My face burned, not with shame but rage. They finally swerved away and the night draped back around me.

I remembered reading about a tactic that eco-warriors had used to save national forests. They dragged fallen trees and other objects from the forest floor into the logging roads, creating blockades. The logging trucks backed out; the forest lived another day.

So I began dragging rocks, branches, and decaying tree trunks into the paths. Some queers looked over at me with raised eyebrows or walked a wide *U* around my mounting fortifications.

We have to bash back, I said. Fuck Giuliani. My exhortations were accompanied by the sound of long branches splashing through fallen leaves.

A queen in a leather trench coat and a shaved head stopped and smiled. Girlfriend, she said, you bangin' on the wasps' nest tonight, ain't you?

I prayed no undercovers would see or hear me, but I didn't stop. Not until I had erected three barricades along a path that was several feet wider than a car. Unplanned, the barricades went from smallest to tallest. The tallest was over eight feet (a fallen tree with an umbrella of intact branches provided the base). Behind it was the gazebo, the place the cops most love to surprise us—that's where group scenes often happen.

Five minutes passed. Some cops in an electric car drove in to start another sweep of the area. They pulled up to the lowest of the barricades and...a crash, a scraping of rock and wood on metal.

Their lights started flashing and the vehicle remained stationary for a full minute before continuing forward. They were heading toward the next barricade.

Other queers stood in clumps, watching, waiting. Some of them snickered.

The cops hit the next barricade without seeing it, the sound of damage much louder. This time, the car didn't move. One of them hit the sirens and must have radioed for backup, because an SUV spun down another path, headed toward the gazebo, lights flashing. The driver slammed the brakes right before the third barricade.

Within five minutes, a sea of red and blue lights pulsed along the peripherals of the Ramble as dozens of backup units arrived. I unchained my bike and pedaled out, laughing. Even if I'd fucked up everyone's cruising for the night, I still felt freer than when I'd arrived.

I keep telling Snake Boy—actually, his name's Ahmed—Thanks man, really, thanks so much, I just totally froze back there. He smiles and rubs my arm and says he's happy we got away. We creep through the shadows. Luckily, so many guys are wandering down paths or moaning in the woods or standing there rubbing their crotches that we should be able to blend.

We walk across an elevated footpath with metal hand railings. Then Ahmed points down into the ravine on the left, and after my eyes adjust, I see, just barely, a steep staircase gouged into the cliffside. We hop the railing and descend the steps into the darkness. At the bottom, we're alone, obscured from almost every angle.

I pull my messenger bag over my head, set it on the moist ground. Then I slide Ahmed's shirt up, suck one of his tight, hard nipples. He massages my scalp, says Oh baby, you're so pretty, look at that hot ass of yours. I trace the back of his right thigh and he grins.

So it's not too long before I'm practically crawling on top of him. I'm chewing his lips. He unbuttons the top of my pants and pushes them down, and there they go again, landing with that same *thunk,* and even in this ravine, the warm air brushes my pelvis and my skin feels so new.

Pebbles tumble down near us. We jump like we just stepped on a live wire with bare feet. The sound of falling pebbles turns into the unmistakable even rhythm of footsteps coming down the staircase. Fuck, fuck, fuck. Pants. Up. Button. I can't get the fucking button to—

I jerk my head up, see a mahogany-skinned man with baggy jeans so low that the fly of his boxers peeks out. His shirt is hooked over his head, bunched up along his shoulders, exposing his worked-out chest muscles.

Keep about your business, he says, reaching up and adjusting the black bandana he wears with the knot tied above his forehead, gangsta-style. I see another guy behind him who's chubby and cute, like someone's kid brother. He wears a football jersey that hangs to his knees.

I glance toward Ahmed and he looks down for a second and then shrugs a Sure, why not. My fingers unclench and my pants, since I never did get them buttoned, drop for the third time tonight. Just have to be more careful, I promise myself. The yellow spandex shorts glow in the semidarkness.

Then the guy with the black bandana saunters toward me and nudges Ahmed away. He reaches out to the small of my back, grabs a fistful of spandex, and tugs it up until I can feel it burrowing into my asscrack. I turn my head to get a better look at him. Up close like this, I can see the details of his tattoos: Christ on a cross, left bicep; a dragon stretching from right pec to over his shoulder. He pulls down his checkered boxers and his cock springs out, pops up once, twice. I swear, even in these shadows, I can see its ropey veins throbbing. Nobody's speaking.

Black Bandana grabs a handful of my dreadlocks and pushes my head forward till my chest is lying against the warm rocks of the stairs and my ass is pointing into the air. He slaps his cock on my lower back several times.

You like that black dick? he says.

I hear the crinkle of plastic and turn around to see him

rolling a condom down his shaft. He slaps his cock on my back again and then spreads my asscheeks and runs it up and down between them. The guy with the football jersey moves a hand around the outside of my hole and I feel the cold jelly wetness of lubrication, so much of it that it oozes down my legs.

Black Bandana smacks my ass. I gasp. My chest stays flat against the staircase. He sticks his cock near my hole and I feel rabbit-thrusts, him just toying with the idea of fucking me. I breathe deep again. He pushes for real this time, but even with all the lube, it's too big. I cry out, forgetting about the cops, the breeze, the other guys around me, everything but that bull's-eye of pain and him saying, Come on, nigga. Open that ass. Open. That. Ass.

I'm white as white but it's so hot that he says that and I don't know why it gets me off but it does. He slides his cock in slow, prying me open, and I'm clenching my asshole, trying to resist 'cause it does hurt but then his pelvis is flush against me. He's in.

My cock lifts and lands back on the stone. I reach down to stroke it but Black Bandana grabs my arm, stops me.

He tightens his abdominals harder and then his thighs start smacking into my ass and my whole body jolts with each smack. Manhattan still hums somewhere in the background and I add my moan to its incessant drone.

Ahmed walks around us, up to the rock stair that my head hovers above. He sits there, legs on either side of me.

Come on, suck it, he says. He sticks his cock in my mouth and I slurp. He rubs the tops of his fingers along my cheek. My body keeps rocking to the cadence of Black Bandana's thrusts. I can't get my mouth moving to the right counter-rhythm. So Ahmed grabs the back of my head and jerks it toward him each time his hips push forward.

I roll my eyes to the left and see the guy in the football jersey jerking off.

My cock is so hard but I still can't grab it 'cause Black Bandana keeps my right arm behind my back and I need the other to stay propped up. My knees feel like they're bruising.

Yeah, nigga, yeah, Black Bandana says. I don't hear anything else anymore and my ass doesn't hurt, it's warm ripples spreading all the way to my head and then even further outward, it's tingles so strong my toes curl, I breathe heavy and steady, and my eyes seal tight like I'm seeing into the beyond. Ahmed keeps rubbing the back of my head and fucking my face. I hear sirens from far away and they're getting closer but we don't stop. I taste the pretzel salt of pre-cum. They can't stop us. They never could.

# THE BOY IN THE MIDDLE

Thom Wolf

The boy was waiting by the east gate of the university, just as we had planned. He stood at the bus stop, slouched against a post, smoking a miniature cigar. He wore a dirty pair of jeans and a navy hooded sweater.

His profile had said he was eighteen but he looked a year or two younger. I considered driving on without stopping but as he *was* waiting outside an adult college I let the age thing go. He looked up as I pulled over, threw his smoke into the gutter and got in the car.

"Hi," he said.

I looked him over carefully. His hair was dark and cut military short. He had deep-set eyes and a small stud pierced his bottom lip. His mouth was slightly uneven and sullen. Kind of cute, I thought, despite the attitude.

"Do you still want this?" I asked.

"Sure I do. I'm here aren't I?"

\* \* \*

Jack was waiting in the living room when I brought the boy home. He was shirtless, a can of beer resting on his hairy belly. His eyes ignited on sight of the youth and he stroked his crotch as a mark of esteem.

The boy said his name was Jared. It seemed to suit. At fifty-five, Jack and I had been together for more years than Jared had been alive. If our age concerned him, it didn't show. From his first contact, an email containing a nude photo, Jared had actively courted us. The details in his emails were explicit, spelling out his need for older men. Much older men. *I want to get fucked,* he claimed; *fisted, double penetrated.* I thought his claims were over the top, just a tease, but the boy persisted until finally, six weeks later, he was here.

"Are you clean, boy?" Jack asked.

The boy answered like a soldier. "Yes, sir."

"Your asshole?"

"Absolutely. Ready for anything."

Satisfied, Jack popped the fly on his jeans, hauling out his big semihard dick. The boy got on his knees and swallowed. Jack put both hands on the back of his head and forced him down. Jared spluttered. I went to the kitchen for a beer. When I came back into the room, Jack was fully stiff and the boy's lips slipped up and down his pole at a constant rhythm. I lingered at the edge of the scene, watching. Jack told him to open his eyes and look at him while he sucked. The boy complied and emerged almost angelic with wide brown eyes, a furrowed brow, and his wet mouth stuffed with cock. Jack's hands remained on his head, guiding the pace.

I knelt behind the boy and slid my hands around him, unfastening his jeans. He wore cheap blue shorts that slipped from his ass with a whisper. He carried a little puppy fat around his rump. His skin was very white and his asscheeks were heavy, dusted with dark hair. His ass was ample in my hands. I opened him, looking into the hairy crack, at the rosy pink hole in the black. Breathing in the savory scent of his butt, I moved closer. His body shuddered when I began to rim him, swirling my tongue around the seam of his asshole, tasting fresh sweat. I slid a hand between his legs, feeling hairy, low-hanging nuts and a small cock that was still soft. I reveled in the youth of his body. It seemed unformed, underdeveloped compared with the flesh I was used to holding.

The lube was in a drawer beside the TV. I slicked up my fingers and started on his ass, sliding one into his warm tract, then quickly working three digits past his ring. Greasing his hot ass, I looked along the line of his spine toward Jack, whose eyes were half lidded as the boy slobbered on his dick. Despite my efforts I couldn't get a fourth finger into his tight snatch, his ring refusing to yield any further, but I was tired of finger-fucking, I was ready for the real thing.

I threw my T-shirt into the room behind me and shucked my jeans over my ass. I fisted another handful of lube over my cock and maneuvred the head into the crack, nudging his sloppy hole. He took the head easily, but his body tensed when I slipped deeper inside. Jack tightened his hold on Jared's head, forcing the boy's face into his lap.

"Take it, you slut. This is what you wanted."

Dick fully inserted, my hips pressed against his fat ass. I held him by the waist, routing him to my cock. We fucked the boy from both ends, stuffing his ass and mouth. I watched as tiny beads of sweat began to form on the smooth white curve of his spine. His ability to take it so passively, without complaint, urged me to go further, harder, faster, rougher. Soon, rivulets of sweat trailed down my own back, prompted by the rapid motion of my hips. His big asscheeks wobbled under the onslaught of my pelvis.

Jack released his grip on the boy's head. "Change places with me," he said. "I want to fuck that."

My stiff cock slipped out of his ass with a slurp, pranging its lubey head against my belly. I sat on the sofa while Jack took a turn mounting the boy's ass. If Jared had any misgivings about sucking a dick that came fresh from his backside, he was not deterred by them. He grabbed my shaft and his mouth went straight down onto it. Jack must have loosened up his throat because the boy had no trouble swallowing me whole.

After several minutes we flipped again. Turning the boy over onto his back, I reentered his ass while Jack squatted over his face and fucked it. The boy took everything we gave without grievance. His body was slack and willing, though his cock didn't show the slightest stiffness. I came first, draining my balls into the soft, warm depths of his bowel. When I was finished, shuddering through the tail of my climax, Jack took my place. He rammed his dick into Jared's come-sloppy ass, churning it over until his own heavy load merged with mine.

Later, the three of us stood at the kitchen door, still in our underwear, smoking. It was a drizzly afternoon and the garden was littered with brown fallen leaves. I was feeling good about the encounter, relaxed in the aftermath of sex. Jack laughed at the boy's miniature cigars and offered him a fat Don Julian. The boy toked on the big cigar, blowing smoke into the garden. He also seemed relaxed, less guarded than before.

"How many older men have you had?" Jack asked him.

"Only one," the boy replied, "besides you two. I used to meet a guy from Durham. He was forty-two. I thought he'd be able to teach me stuff, but he didn't. Not really. He just wanted to cuddle and fuck all the time."

I laughed. "And you don't?"

"Sure I do, but I want more than that. I want a man who'll use me. I want to be his boy."

"What does that mean?"

"I just want sex. I don't want dinner and DVDs. I want to be fucked, roasted, as many cocks as I can get. You know, like we did today. You guys didn't want to get to know me. You just wanted to fuck me." He exhaled a great cloud of smoke. "That's cool, 'cause it's what I want too."

"You're a strange kid," I said.

"Don't analyze me, just fuck me. Do what you want. Fuck me, fist me, stuff massive dildos up my ass; whatever you want to do. I told you, that's what I want."

I stifled a smile. His talk was the stuff of porn and overly imaginative forum chat. I guess he had constructed a fantasy image for himself—as an uberbottom—and was desperately trying to live up to his creation. I imagined he had an XTube profile and a whole gallery of videos recorded on his webcam. I'd seen plenty of boys like him online, spreading their asscheeks and stuffing themselves with every imaginable instrument. It was hot and entirely ridiculous at the same time. Silly boy, and yet his naivete was somehow endearing.

One week later I picked him up from the same spot. He trotted to the car and greeted me with an enthusiastic smile. He appeared different, brighter, more assured. The weather had made an unseasonable turn for the better and, although it was November, he wore a baggy pair of shorts that hung halfway down his ass and a tight, sleeveless T-shirt.

"How's it going?" he chirped. "Got something exciting for me today?"

Jack and I had talked long and hard before inviting him back. Jared was a horny little piece, and as a couple of old farts we were flattered, but there was something about him that raised doubts. I had serious reservations about getting involved. Perhaps it was the artifice of his person, the carefully studied behavior. We didn't know him; I doubted we ever would, no matter how many times we fucked him. We were old men. It was pleasing to think a young boy wanted us so keenly, but I had a niggling suspicion that he was trouble, and at our age we didn't need that.

I took him straight to the bedroom, where Jack was waiting in a loose pair of pants tented by his dick. Jared undressed in a hurry, flinging his clothes into the corner of the room. He wore a black jockstrap and kept his white socks on. It was a look I'm sure he'd lifted from porn. He dived straight onto the bed, releasing Jack's dick and going down on it like cannibal. He took it right to the root, deep-throating on the first pass. Jack closed his eyes and surrendered to Jared's lips. I undressed slowly, watching, listening to the wet slobbering sounds from the bed. Jack looked like he was enjoying himself. Despite my reservations I was hard before I slipped my shorts to the floor.

I got on the bed and grabbed hold of Jared's short hair. I dragged his mouth off Jack's dick and shoved him down on my own. He gasped and snuffled but his lips were around the fat root in seconds. I let him have it hard, holding his head in place while I rammed my cock deep into his throat. The boy gagged and made startling animal noises but I refused to release my hold.

"This is what you wanted," I said, fucking his face with an angry passion, surprising myself.

When I finally relented the boy sat back on his haunches, gasping for breath. Saliva drooled from his small chin, dripping down his neck and heaving chest. Jack got into a kneeling position beside me. I could feel the tension in his body, the tightly coiled excitement. He grabbed the boy's head and gave him a session of similar treatment, holding his face, sinking his cock into the depths of his throat. After a while we began to alternate, moving his face forcibly between our dicks. He had just a moment to catch his breath before we took our turns reaming his sweet mouth. It all felt wrong but I was *so* turned on, more than I had been in years. It was exploitation, dirty, almost like rape. I had to remind myself that this was exactly what he'd asked for.

My reservations were insignificant beside my zeal for the boy. I left Jack to his mouth while I started work on his ass. The boy had been perfectly explicit in describing the things he wanted us to do to him. I intended to give him just what he wanted and in the process learn how much of him was genuine, and how much was artifice. I lubed his butthole, paying attention to its tightness and size. It wasn't long before I was able to slip three fingers effortlessly back and forth through his sphincter, like a bolt in a well-oiled lock. His pink opening flourished and unfurled around my hand. When he was hot and loose, I opened the drawer beneath the bed, where Jack and I kept the toys.

*No point starting small with a kid like this*, I told myself, selecting a medium-sized dildo with an enjoyably fat head. The boy gasped and raised his hips higher when I introduced the wide tip to his butt. The next toy to stuff him was a corpulent black dildo with an unfeasibly thick girth. The boy made a sound that could have been a cry, if it weren't muffled by the meat in his mouth. I had to put some weight behind the base of the toy and force it through the resistance of his ass. Just as I began to think that this one was beyond him, his sphincter gave way and the fattest part of the dildo went in. I followed through, pushing the entire length deep into him. I fucked him with the big one, churning his ass into a sloppy mess, and when I finally withdrew, his hole was squelchy and beautifully slack.

I mounted him then, slipping my cock into his welcoming bowel, and despite the slackness of his hole, it was not long before I ejaculated a huge, gooey load into his ass. My come trickled from his anus when I pulled out and ran in a slow trail across his balls.

Jared wanted to return the following weekend. We concocted an excuse and declined him. The following week we were out of town, visiting friends in the country. It was almost a month before we agreed to see him again. As before, we'd considered the implications of having him over. Did we really want to involve ourselves further? My reservations lingered but there was something in the tone of his emails, the explicit detail of his text messages, which aroused me and made me want him. That third afternoon was much like those that preceded it; we ravaged his lips, forcing both dicks into his mouth at once. We fingered, fucked, and dildoed his hole. Just as we had with his mouth, we pushed both our cocks into his asshole. The boy screamed at the double penetration as he straddled my hips. Jack shoved in from behind while I was already in him. The boy's face contorted with the effort, mouth wide open, eyes shut tight. His small body lay between us, tight against my chest. I kissed his twisted lips as we fucked.

Jack and I took Viagra that day. Once we had both come inside him, it took just a short while to rouse ourselves back to a state of excitement. Jared lay back across the bed and we fucked him long and slow from both ends, taking it in turn to pillage his mouth and anus. His butt smelled strongly of spunk as we churned. He farted afterward, spurting the white gunk onto our sheets. He spread his legs wide and we scooped the come back into his hole. Afterward we lifted him into the bath and pissed all over him. He turned his face into the amber streams, opening his mouth, bathing in the shower. The boy smiled and piss poured from the corners of his mouth.

Our afternoons with Jared became an odyssey as we explored the limits of his body. The boy was never anything more than passive. He rarely got hard as we delved into his ass, and he never ejaculated. We put everything imaginable up his ass: toys, snooker balls, food. We gave him enemas of beer and milk and applauded the spectacular fountains that erupted from his hole. Once, with several loads of come inside him, he squatted and dumped the hot white stuff into a bowl, before pouring the butt-fermented spunk down his throat. Nothing was too much for him. He had no limits. Each day when we were done with him, he asked when he could come back. "Not another week," he complained, "that's too long. Can't I come over tomorrow?" I refused to acquiesce to his demands and kept a minimum of seven days between our meetings.

If he had another man on the go during that time, he didn't mention it and we didn't ask. On reflection we knew very little about him. He went to college but where he came from was a mystery. He didn't talk about friends or interests. He didn't talk about anything except the things he wanted us to do to him.

After a couple of months I began to lose interest. Despite the wild experiments, sex with him became routine. His passivity was predictable, boring. If he displayed any passion, any physical response to the things we did, it might have been different. But he took it all without comment or reaction.

I began to spank him, with my hand at first until I bought a flat leather paddle to use on his smooth white flesh. I used it hard, beating his rump until it smarted. The boy made all the right noises, gasping, crying, though I noticed there were no tears in his eyes. His reaction, like every other, was artifice.

"Same time next week?" he asked. "You gonna pick me up at the usual place?"

We were in my car, just the two of us, as I delivered him to the bus stop. He had a hand on the door, ready to bound off.

"No," I said at last. "Next week won't do."

His pretty face fell. "The week after then?"

"I don't think so. I think it's time we took a break."

"What?" his bottom lips thrust forward. "Don't you want me?"

The answer was no, but I broke it to him gently. "Jack and I are a couple. For the sake of our own relationship, we can't keep doing this. I'm sorry, Jared. It's not your fault, but you have to respect what we have. I'm afraid it's over."

It wasn't over. His messages, via email and text, continued. He sent photos of himself and short films recorded on his webcam. I deleted each message without response. The only way he would get the message was to cease all contact. After a while the frequency of his messages began to dwindle. Jack and I returned to a monogamous kind of normality. We didn't feel the need to prove our manliness or desirability by having sex with much younger guys. I continued to feel uneasy about the affair. I wasn't proud but in time I began to forget. It was easy to pretend it never happened.

Until the doorbell rang one Saturday evening in March. Jack was making dinner while I worked on my laptop in the study. The bell rang insistently, quickly followed by a rapid hammering. I knew it was Jared before I answered.

He swayed on the doorstep when I answered.

"Hey man," he pushed straight through into the living room. "Where've you been? I've been waiting for you."

He smelled of beer. But there was more to his behavior than alcohol. He was completely out of it. His pupils were black holes, his expression crazed and distant. He shucked his jacket off onto a chair and began to hitch his T-shirt over his head. His body was noticeably thinner than before. He'd lost muscle tone and his rib cage was painfully visible. I noticed a profusion of white stains on his pants.

"What are you doing?" I asked. Jack came through from the kitchen, his face stony.

The boy laughed, a sharp, hysterical sound. "I'm here to get laid," he drawled, unbuckling his belt. "Come on guys, do me! Do me right fucking now! Fuck my ass."

"I don't think so," I picked up the clothes he had discarded and threw them back at him.

"Come on. You want me. You always want me. My ass is good, good and nasty. I got a butt load of come in there. Nice and sloppy for you."

I stared at him, appalled, as he shucked his jeans down his skinny legs. His cock was a worm in an unruly nest of pubes, white and wasted. He came over to me, grabbed my hand and forced it onto his dick. It was cold and lifeless. I recoiled.

"What are you on, you idiot?"

He giggled and turned to Jack. "You wanna fuck me, don't you Daddy?"

"No. Get out." Jack's tone was uncompromising. It seemed to get through to the boy's addled mind. Jared's face slackened. He wavered in the middle of room. I thought for a moment that he was going to puke.

I offered to drive him home.

"Home," he repeated, and the word seemed to have no

meaning on his lips. "Fuck you, you pair of cunts." He pulled his pants up, struggling with the fastenings. "If you don't wanna fuck me there are plenty of guys who do. Hundreds of guys." He retrieved his T-shirt and jacket and cursed us as he dressed.

I stepped aside as he staggered to the door. I looked at Jack. "We can't let him go out, not like that."

Jack shrugged. Jared had already gone. "He got himself into that state; he can get himself out of it."

Outside there was no sign of the boy. I searched the street in both directions but he had vanished. As I returned to the house and locked the door, I hoped, a little guiltily, that he was gone for good.

# UNDERGROUND OPERATOR

Andrew McCarthy

Nowhere in New York City is July's inescapable heat more viscerally punishing than below ground, where the atmospheric pressure rises with the descent into the subway. The potent odor of decay and fermented urine, occasionally peppered with bleach or ammonia by maintenance staff, offers little comfort to the unfortunate traveler who is eager to be elsewhere. Worst are evening rush hours, when trains are packed with fatigued commuters, collectively worn down by the day's work and the unforgiving humidity.

Even subway sounds are assaulting: the unintelligible squawk box announcements, the high-pitched gnashing of metal wheels on curving rails, the thunderous rattle of train bodies squeezing their rectangular shapes through winding tunnels. Before a train arrives at a station with its familiar screeching, ironically signaling a relief from some of the subway's other sensory hostilities, platform inhabitants contemplate their abilities to overcome the suffering inherent with waiting for and riding the train.

Will I find a newspaper on the platform bench so I have something to read, or use to wave warm air from side to side in an attempt to cool down? Is there any water left in the bottle in my bag? Do I have a rag to wipe the sweat off of my face, or to slide under my shirt to sponge off my damp back? When the train finally comes, will I get a seat? Most importantly: will the train be air-conditioned? The answer must always be yes in order to preserve sanity.

Regardless of the journey's length, it will never be easy or luxurious. Once I'm on the train, there is no shortage of nuisances, starting with the barrage of advertisements, to which only the blind possess immunity. Portable music players, intended to shield their owners from the subway's annoying sound effects, are turned up to inappropriate volumes, creating their own unwelcome environmental disturbances. Numerous are the loud, inane conversations of callous adults who should know better than to be so tactless. As for the ever-present boisterous adolescents, they could care less about socially appropriate behavior in public spaces. Panhandlers and subway preachers transgress boundaries further than do rib-poking shoulder bags; their grief, desperation, and diatribes remind us how much we want to be home, where privacy is guaranteed.

Fulton Street train station is the busiest subway complex in lower Manhattan, linking four train lines and serving nearly three hundred thousand passengers daily. Of those four train lines, the BMT is the least busy, and boasts only one real transportation asset: the M train. Starting in Middle Village, Queens, the M makes a few stops in lower Manhattan, and then runs into southern Brooklyn, but only until about eight o'clock at night. Afterward, passengers can take the J train, which shares a portion of its route with the M, running from Queens into Manhattan. The big difference is that the J terminates one stop after Fulton Street, in the sleepy financial district. Late at night, J trains arriving at the deserted downtown Fulton Street station carry few passengers, and fewer, if any, people wait to board the train. People still wait on the platform, but not necessarily for the train.

Long after crowded subway cars are vacated by passengers who think themselves entitled to imaginary and invented private space, the intersections of public and personal intimacy are explored on the platform. And this is where my story begins.

The Brooklyn-bound #2 train I was on pulled into Fulton Street around ten o'clock. I got out and navigated through the maze of passages and staircases to the downtown J train. Moving slowly through the palpable heat of the quiet station, I looked around and saw no one. The platform arcs in a way that leaves its northern section obscured, and that is where I headed, hoping to find a piece. As I approached the end of the platform, a figure became visible from behind one of the many steel-beam columns that run from the floor to the ceiling of the station. As I got closer, a well-kept, stocky brother revealed himself.

I eased my stride, checking him out as I walked to the column behind the one he was leaning on. My man was in his late thirties, shorter and heavier then me—about five foot eight inches tall, weighing about one hundred seventy pounds—light-brown-skinned, with a mustache and shaved head. Dark blue jeans wrapped tightly around his hefty thighs, and a thin, sky-blue basketball tank top hung from his shoulders, draped over his burly torso. Large white vinyl letters spelled out RIM ROKKA. His arms were big, and any muscular definition was subtle. This man was undeniably hot.

Positioned opposite him, my back against the metal girder,

I reached my right hand down to grab my crotch while my left hand rubbed my chest through my fitted tank top. The resonant buzz of the fluorescent lights above characterized the tense contemplation that filled the next few seconds before either of us made a move. Finally, his thick fingers pulled at the bulge in his jeans. This single gesture answered my greeting with affirmation, and I stepped nearer.

Standing in front of him now, both of us still pawing at our dicks, I ran my free hand across his meaty chest, excited by the firmness and impressive size of his broad pecs. He narrowed his eyes and opened his mouth, sighing as I brushed his stiffening nipples. My hand found its way below his shirt, sliding up his smooth hard belly to his chest, where my fingers rolled his right nipple, then his left. Leaning into him, grinding my waist into his, my eyes caught the first sight of his naked upper body as he raised his shirt over his head to lay it across the back of his neck, signaling his commitment to this encounter. His robust muscular build, covered in a thick layer of skin, seemed natural; definitely sexier than a gym-manufactured sculpture.

I made sure that there was no one else around by craning my neck to look past the column we were hiding behind. My man's hand gently pulled me back, drawing my head lower to his chest. My lips parted as they made contact and my tongue flicked across the tips of his nipples. Cradling me in his burly forearm, he guided my head back and forth as my mouth remoistened the dried sweat that flavored his skin salty. I lifted my tank top to give him access to my nipples, which he rubbed and made firm. He then freed my growing dick from my jeans and dug out my balls with two fingers, massaging them before palming my cock. He spoke for the first time. "Damn. You got some big dick, Pa. You gonna break me off a piece of this?" His voice was as deep as his intent. Smiling, and feeling up his trade through the fabric of his jeans, I replied "Hell yeah! Let's get to work."

He squeezed as much of my dick as could fit in his hand, hardening me further. Shaking his head, his eyes locked on me as he unfastened his belt and loosened his pants. I pulled down his jeans and boxers to find his already-hard dick and balls nestled between his massive legs. He was smaller then me—about five inches long—and had a tight foreskin that pulled back from a shiny pink head. Both our dicks curved upward, but my fat head was his focus. Crouching down, my man lifted my low-hanging nuts to meet his lips, sucking them into his mouth one by one. His mustache crushed into the base of my dick as I bounced its head against his jaw, letting him know what was next.

Shorty repositioned himself and was kneeling before me on the filthy platform floor. He was not here to waste time, which was perfect for me, because I meant business. I pushed my crotch into his face as he sucked my balls. "Harder. Suck 'em harder," I instructed as I cupped his head in my hand, pulling his face into my groin. A cherry-flavored condom was fished from my pocket and rolled down to the base of my dick. I receded to get enough room for brandishing my trade, showing off the piece he was going to eat. My dick bobbed in the air before he took hold of it, pulling me closer as his mouth and eyes opened wide.

His lips and tongue ushered my cock into his wet mouth, and the intensity of the pleasure matched the density of the hot humid air. He got me harder by rotating his head from left to right as he sucked. His hand wrapped around my cock and followed his mouth up and down my piece while his tongue licked my shaft. On the way down, he'd remove his hand so that he could take all of me inside of him until his mustache blended with my pubic hair. Increasing the speed and strength with which he sucked, my man grabbed the back of my legs for leverage as he jerked back and forth. His head nodded furiously up and down, and I writhed on the platform, desperately trying to keep my groaning to a minimum.

Suddenly my dick popped out of the cocksucker's mouth as he coughed and spit, then climbed up off his knees. Standing in front of me, his chest lifting with heavy breathing, he panted, "Fuck me, yo." He pulled his pants down past his knees as he turned around and bent over, bracing himself on the column in front of us. Brother man stretched his arm back and pulled his left cheek out of the way, exposing his hairless hole to the air and to my throbbing cock. He was already wet and opening up, inviting me to slide in. It's a good thing I packed a bottle of lube with the condoms I was carrying, because I like to get up in a man when his ass is sloppy and juicy. After lubing my dick, I grabbed his other asscheek and closed in on his hole, pushing the knobby head of my cock inside, then plunging in until our legs smacked together.

"*Ugh!*" The words were exhaled in a rush as he arched his back, all an involuntary response to the sensation of sudden penetration. "Yeah, Pa, I got some dick for you," I said as I pulled all the way out and rammed back into his ass. My man let go off his asscheek and reached back to pull on mine, driving me further inside him. He pushed back on me as I boned him with long steady thrusts. We kept at this rhythm, and the sound of our bodies banging together echoed off the tiled walls.

In defiance of our public setting's limitations, he began to wail loudly as I repeatedly jammed my dick into his fleshy ass. Our sexual transformation of the train platform heightened the urgency of our horny aggressions. Bending over him, I laid my chest against his broad sweaty back, and wrapped my hand over his mouth to keep him quiet. My fingers were sucked into his mouth as he grunted: "Fuck me! Fuck me!" His hand still clung to me but had slid down my leg, his fingers digging deeper into my hamstrings. Both of us pulled on each other, frenzied with lust. "Take this dick, man. Take this dick!" I demanded as my hips pounded against him. He flexed the muscles in his ass, squeezing my dick and tickling all of my nerve endings.

In his current bent-over position, and with both of us throttled by sensations, neither of us noticed that we were not alone. Walking up the platform toward us was a guy I'd seen cruising before, immediately recognizable by his dark complexion and Trinidadian flag handkerchief tying back his shoulder-length dreadlocks. I kept fucking so as not to alarm my partner.

The newcomer arrived, proceeding with a cautious pace, and stopped a few feet away to watch. He looked around thirty, slim, and roughly six feet tall. A light beard complemented his handsome angular features and conveyed a sense of appealing masculinity. He was wearing gray sweat shorts with a matching zip-up short-sleeved shirt that was embroidered in red with a simple graffiti-style crown across the chest; it was the logo for the hip-hop clothing company PNB, whose acronym had many original meanings, such as "Post No Bills" and "Proud Nubian Brothers." Tonight, it meant "Poppa Needs Bicho."

Triniman's dick was already raising the right leg of his shorts by the time his hand grabbed hold of his trade and gently shook it. I raised an eyebrow and jerked my head in my direction, inviting him to come over. As he did, the guy I was dicking down saw him and stood up to better view the dude and assess the situation. Just then, we heard the train as it screeched through the tunnel leading into the station. Quickly, hard-ons were tucked away and clothing was pulled back into place as we dispersed.

From our separate locations, we instinctively took inventory of the passengers on the passing J train, looking for uniformed cops or transit workers who might get out and investigate our reasons for loitering since we had not boarded the train. One woman with a large plastic shopping bag exited the middle of the train and left the platform, presumably to transfer to one of the other subway lines. No one got on the train, and only the three of us remained. Before the last few cars of the J snaked out of the southern end of the station, we were already positioning ourselves to resume our tryst.

The dread's bulge was still present, and both me and the guy I was fucking were eager to sexplore his package. He unzipped his shirt and its two sides parted, uncovering a hairy chest and solid, worked-out stomach. The bottom again raised his jersey, and my tank top also came up. Fingers tweaked nipples, and hands fondled growing dicks through our pants. I liberated my dick and started to pull at it. The heavyset guy unbuckled and lowered his jeans, and bent over to start sucking on the Trini's dick, which came out for the first time. His cock was fat like a cucumber and about nine inches long. A thick foreskin hung over the tip, laced by ropelike veins, as much of his body was. He started tugging at my dick while I played with his nipples. The light-skinned dude slobbered on the new cock for only half a minute before turning around to take it up his horny ass. I gave the baller a condom to put on, and they started fucking.

As Trini's dick pushed into the beckoning hole, the bottom began moaning loud enough to get us all busted. I wrapped up my piece in a mint-flavored hood and maneuvered in front of him so he could give me head. This shut him up. He reached for my leg to brace himself as he started beating his meat, and I steadied his shoulders. The blow job was messy and not as methodical as before since his concentration was on his back getting banged out. Drool leaked out of my sucker's mouth as he gasped for air. He intermittently choked on my dick as the stud plowing him forced him forward every time they crashed together.

"Fuck that ass!" I hissed to turn them on more.

"Yuh dun know," the Trini confirmed in an accent as thick as curry stew from Sunday night cook-up as he juked the man in front of him harder. Sweat began to form on the top's skin. I wanted a taste of the glistening sweat droplets in his body hair, so I arched my back over the man between us and planted my face in the Trinbagoan's bulky tits. Surrounded by coils of black hair, his nipples stiffened inside my mouth as my tongue wiggled over them one at a time. His breath blew forcefully past my ear as he fucked our bottom brother. The top's hand buried my head in his muscular chest as his momentum grew faster. The guy getting screwed was moaning in high pitches, almost crying, getting ready to cum as his body jerked powerfully. He yelped as his whole body shook with the fury of busting his nut. The spray of his gray-white cum flew everywhere, coating my lower legs and the cement floor.

Resuming normal posture, the bottom retrieved a washcloth from his back pocket and wiped off his sweat-soaked body. After his breathing normalized and he gathered himself, he smiled at us and said, "This shit was mad hot. One." Then he bounced from the scene. This left me and the man with the big bamboo. He'd taken off the condom and tossed it into the tracks, and was now playing with his long cock, rolling his foreskin back and forth on his big dickhead. His trade bowed downward and curved to the left, and was still hard. He laid his hand on my shoulder and pressured me downward to blow him. "Your time to taste de cocoa," he asserted.

Squatting in front of him, I stretched a condom over his piece while I licked the insides of his hairy thighs, passing my tongue over the many veins detailing his skin's surface. With one hand wound around the base of his shaft, I opened my mouth and wrapped my lips and tongue around his glans, sliding my mouth down as far as I could go until he hit the back of my throat. I repeated this a few times before swallowing his cock whole, gagging on its girth and length. "Mmmmm…" he groaned. I looked up at him as I brought my lips all the way to the base of his cock again. He grasped the sides of my head and started to fuck my face. The strength of his motions almost knocked me down, so I slid my hands up beneath his shorts, laying my palms on his quads to steady myself.

After a couple of minutes, my man pulled me up so we stood face-to-face. My heart was racing. In one movement, the dread cocked his head, parted his lips, and we started kissing. Our tongues braided together in a passionate electric charge. I closed my eyes and opened up to this sexy stranger, forgetting about the stifling heat, the decrepit plaster ceiling falling apart above our heads, and the dangers we flirted with tonight in the subway—and every day—for being gay. We ignored the threat of hostility, and accepted our vulnerability by creating this plea-surable intimacy behind enemy lines. Fuck the police. We were going to fuck each other.

Arms searched for flesh unvisited by touch, eager to deliver affections. His hands found my backside and I found his interest. He started to pry at the opening of my ass, and I wet his fingers with lube. Gently, he entered me with an index finger and began massaging my insides as we continued kissing. I gripped his cock and lubed it up, because he wanted to lay some pipe, and it had to fit with ease. Our tongues untangled as he pulled away to spit on his cock. "I'm gonna mash up this bamsee, boy!" he declared.

"Ya promise?" I teased.

"Fuh true."

I turned around and bent over, then backed onto his piercing fat cock. The initial pain of the penetration flashed up my spine, but soon was replaced with a flood of ecstasy. No balling in recent memory felt this good. "Yeah," he breathed heavily as he jammed himself faster into my ass. I stretched my arms back to twist his nipples between my fingers, letting go when his chest pushed into my back as he folded himself over on top of me. Then one of my hands grabbed the column that we hid behind while the other worked my dick.

He gripped my waist roughly, pounding his hips against me, and I took all of him inside of me. My nerves were more stimulated each time he forced his cock into my ass. "Damn, this dick is good. Pump that ass, Pa!" I half whispered. Brother man kissed me as he massaged my prostate with his strokes. His tongue ran up my neck and into my ear. His mouth was on my ear as he asked, "You like this cockstand, baby?"

"Hell yeah! Give me all that dick. No mercy on my ass."

The grindsman let go of my waist, and hugged me with great strength, grunting as he bucked more powerfully than before. He rushed into me faster and harder, and built up so much speed that I began biting his arm to keep from screaming out loud. My ass surely was going to ache from the beating, but the sensory overload felt so good. I tilted my pelvis upward to provide better access to my hole, and I jacked my dick. "You got some cum for me? I wanna see you shoot it." I managed to get the words out between gasps for air. My man loosened his grip on my shoulders and climbed off my back. He yanked off the condom to beat his flesh raw. My mouth instinctively found itself on his nipples, and I pumped my own cock as we both edged toward the explosion of orgasm.

"Oh!" He strained to drag the breath from the depths of his spasming frame as he busted. His brawny arms and hairy pecs tensed as he heaved forward, pressing himself into my side while he beat his dick faster and tighter. Streams of cum shot across the platform and down into the darkness of the tracks. The end of his load dribbled down his fist and into the wiry black pubic hair at the base of his thick cock, now resplendent with the iridescent liquid. I furiously jerked my dick until I came, lacing his stomach with liquid pearls that streamed down the contour of his tight abdomen.

I pinned the dread against the I-beam, our moist bodies connecting in the heat. We kissed and squeezed each other with exhilaration until the familiar smell of burned diesel fuel from a work train began to fill the air. Both of us scrambled to assemble ourselves before the train made it through the tunnel and into the station. I wiped off my hands on my chest and legs before lowering my shirt and pulling up my pants. My partner in sex crime rubbed his hands together in an attempt to dry them off before zipping up. He slapped my ass and grinned as we left the scene.

The soot-covered yellow work train winded through the station after blowing its deafening horn twice. Black exhaust clouds billowed into the air. The train was comprised of about eight cars, most of which were flatbeds that carried dozens of dumpsters. The containers were full of trash that had been collected from all of the other stations along the J line. The poignant smell of rot was overwhelming.

I asked where my man was headed, and he said he was going to Brooklyn on the #2 train. "Me too," I said with a feeling of serendipity. He facetiously asked if it was because I was coming back to his place. The answer would always be yes.

# MY BOY TUESDAY

Arden Hill

He needed a name so I named him Tuesday. Tuesday for the day we met in Professor Alice Adams' section of Shakespeare's Women. I was wearing my hair blond and blue then, so of course he noticed me when he walked in the door, though I have no doubt he would have, even if I'd tried to blend in. Blending in is one of the few things I don't excel at. It is an art I choose not to explore. Tuesday was wearing worn brown pants, both knees reinforced with bright green patches. They said to me, "Hello, I kneel down a lot," and so I smiled at them before following the slouchy lines of his body up to a subdued green sweater, solid not striped, soft and patchless. He had a sweet face and when I looked down at my watch I noted he was three minutes late for class. I fantasized about punishing him for this, slapping him hard. And when he became hard enough, I would tie his right hand to his ankles and tell him to make himself come for me with his left one. I would reward him for this act.

When Tuesday came to class that first day, he tucked his

backpack quietly under the chair in front of him, a chair only feet away from mine, so I could see the small pink triangle he'd pinned to the bag's zipper, and the red ribbon that was tied around the zipper. I remember licking my lips and smiling. It's always easier when they know they're gay. I've spent too many semesters with football players sucking my cock, their massive shoulder muscles heaving as they weep salt tears over my come and their spit. When they can breathe again they always say the same thing. "Tristan, man, I think I might be gay. I really liked that. I really liked sucking you off." If I'm not in a bad mood I tell them it was okay, but if I'm pissy, and I mean pissy about anything that happened that day—lousy parking, a dull class, a cold cup of coffee—I tell them, "Well you might be gay now, you big faggot, but that blow job just turned me straight." Those big boys don't wear my collar. They call me by my name. I don't officially top them but it's always there to some degree, and it was there even in the beginning when I was the one down on the floor. When I'm mean to lovers that aren't bottoms they leave and don't come back. Fine. If I'm mean to Tuesday, he might cry a little but I'm sure he'd roll over and stick his ass up in the air for me to cane, or fuck, or just stare at until he wiggles and moans and I decide to be nice.

I can relate to boys like Tuesday, or rather I can remember what it was like to assume that position. I was nineteen. My lover was twenty-six. "Hey boy," he said, "I want to teach you something." He pushed my arms out past my head and jerked back on my ankles until they were next to his knees. The lube was cold when he stuck his finger into my ass but by the time he worked his dick in it was warm, almost burning. "Oh you like that you little slut," he said and he reached for his belt, the one I'd taken off with my teeth earlier in the evening. He hit me twenty-five times across each shoulder. I imagined his hand holding the belt. No. I imagined my hand on the leather. When he had me count out loud I heard the numbers as though it were his voice speaking and I smiled between each word. He told me thank him and I did, though he had no idea what I was thanking him for.

The next night he learned what I'd gathered from his lesson. He said I could tie him up if I wanted. I did, and I did it with the cuffs and joiners he'd used on me earlier. I whipped him lightly and he moaned, his mouth falling open with each flick of leather across his skin. I tightened the restraints and he looked up at me with surprise but delight. I put on a glove and pushed two fingers into him. His dick rose up. I could almost hear it humming. "Oh you like that you little slut," I growled. He gave me a cocky sort of smile before I shoved the gag in his mouth. I put in more fingers and he rocked on my hand. "Now that you're in a position to listen," I said, "our relationship is going to be different and if you're not up for that difference our relationship is going to be over." I undid the gag so he could whisper, "Yes Sir."

I put the gag back in and told him that I'd been thinking about what I did and did not like in bed. I told him he was not going to be allowed to touch my cock. Well, not with his hands at least. Before this moment I endured the feel of my silk underpants shifting to sandpaper as clumsy hands rubbed me through denim. Once my pants were off, too many lovers groped me, tugging and pulling until I was hard but hurting. I put up with it because I liked what happened next, when they thought they had warmed me up enough to lick my dick lightly with the tips of their tongues. I like to be taken on the tongue like a thick wafer, one that does not dissolve but still induces someone to murmur Jesus. I like to spill down a throat. I slipped out the gag and thrust into him, showing him. He swallowed and when

I pulled out he thanked me. I realized then other things I liked: downcast eyes, the strands of hair that fall across the forehead after someone has exerted himself.

Tuesday had run down the hallway in an attempt to make it to class on time. His black bangs were wet. There was a damp curl twisting down the collar of his shirt. I watched him and took notes on Shakespeare's women and my own soon-to-be boy both. I could imagine him on his knees while I, dressed in a gown, lifted up layer after layer of fabric until there was nothing between my cock and his mouth but silk. I would bind his hands first. I would write what I liked on notes that I would not let him read until class. I would have him sit in a different spot, to my left and ahead just a bit so I could watch him read but it would still be clear we were not equals, not in the bedroom, not in any room.

The professor asked a question and Tuesday's slim hand shot up. *Eager*, I remarked to myself, and when Tuesday spoke I liked the tones of his answer. His voice cracked a little on the name Titania, and I knew I wanted him to wear glitter and answer my questions, ending each sentence with a slight and cracking "Sir." The professor looked pleased, which indicated to me that Tuesday is a good reader. I am a good writer. I know this is going to work out. He shifted in his chair a bit and turned around as though my gaze had weight. He looked at me then looked down. He knew from the beginning where this was going. Tuesday was a very bright boy.

After class Tuesday wandered over to my desk. Although articulate with literature, he seemed shy about practical matters, so I told him to come over to my apartment on Wednesday. I took his hand and wrote my address on the back of it. I did not ask for his address. We did not exchange names or numbers. I was certain he'd show up and if he didn't, well I knew where to find him, and I've noticed other boys in this class who I could entice over, boys whose bruises would make Tuesday sorry he did not accept what I offered. I am not stingy, but careful, with my kindnesses.

Tuesday put on his backpack and promised to arrive at my place on time. I wrote *seven* on his wrist. Black ink over the blue of his veins. He smiled, and since I am careful with my compliments I did not tell him that his mouth is perfect. As he walked out I noticed that his ass matches it beautifully. I'd like to fill his ass and his mouth at the same time. I have the evening to decide what will go in each hole. I briefly wonder if Tuesday has a preference and suspect that I will learn. What I will do with that knowledge, I haven't decided. I imagine him grateful. I imagine him suffering. In both circumstances, Tuesday's cheeks are wet with tears and his naked chest is crossed with claw marks.

I like my nails long. Sometimes I paint them with slightly black-tinged gloss so that they shine like talons. Once, when I was at the counter of the grocery store preparing to pay for a package of strawberries, the scruffy man looked at my hands and not my face. He said, "That will be three dollars, Miss." Slightly amused, I responded, "Here you go," as I handed him the bills. "Oh," he gasped looking up, "I thought you were a woman." I pulled the berries from his hands and hissed, "If you were paying attention you would have realized I'm a goddess." I strode out before he could respond.

Everyone has his kink. Mine has a feminine bent. "Don't even think of calling me anything other than Sir," I tell the boys as I take off my panties. Anyone who looks skeptical earns an hour in my drag closet with the instruction not to come out until he is beautiful. Then I take him out for a night on the town. I put on the corresponding clothes, a three-piece suit with my father's favorite tie. We look like a het couple so I buy the girl/boy dinner. I have her/him eat out my ass for dessert.

I think about Tuesday while I am making myself dinner. I am hungry and hungry makes me horny. Something about satiation causes the wires in my brain to cross so that after I fuck a boy, after I come inside him emptying a cock full of cream into his body, I myself feel full. I no longer crave anything but, perhaps, to watch the boy clean himself off with a warm wet rag. With the jocks I've fucked there is no ritual. I send them home immediately after and I do not care how they brush their teeth or scrub their asses raw in the shower. I've been called a bitch on more than one occasion. "Frigid bitch," was the phrase used by the last quarterback after he told me that he loved me and I told him that I wasn't interested in fucking him anymore. He called me frigid and I watched my come cool on his chest.

My thoughts about Tuesday are more tender. I make three portions of tomato sauce, one for me to eat tonight and the other two for us to share on Wednesday. I want him to watch me eat and feel hungry before it is his turn. I want to hand-feed this one. I want to play sweet master, for a while. A mediocre top once told me, "You can't top someone if you're serving them food." I liked neither his phrasing nor his twitchy eyes. I assured him it could be done and pointed out that he didn't deserve for me to prove it to him. Instead, I invited his favorite submissive play partner over and tied him up in my shower. I washed him outside and in. He wept when the water ran cold. I commanded him not to tremble while I patted him dry so gently that he ached to press his hard cock into the towel and hump it until he came but I never let him come. I dressed him up and set him at the dinner table. With one hand, I grasped his throat. With the other, I fed him small bites of vegetable lasagna. I chewed each bite first and, when he looked thirsty, I put water in my mouth and spat it into his. He didn't play with that top again, a decision I'm sure was influenced by his encounter with me. Everyone has his kink and I have a talent for turning people on to mine.

I don't think about Tuesday again until I am bathing. I've poured in a small amount of bubble bath and the white sides of the tub are as smooth and slick as I imagine the head of his cock will be. The water gradually warms the enamel and I push my back down against the bottom. My cock swells and breaks the surface of the water. It bursts bubbles and I fixate on Tuesday's ass, how I want to ease in while he pants at the difficulty of having me there. I haven't seen him around, which means that he is a freshman and, although he has a pink triangle on his bag, the button is new enough that it may have just been put on. He is pretty, but then so are boy bands. I suppose it would not have been difficult for him to be read as straight in high school. Even if people suspected he was gay, he is the kind of pretty that rivals a girl's good looks. Most guys are too scared to ask a boy like that out on a date much less get their dicks into him.

While it is highly likely that young Tuesday is a virgin, I find it impossible to believe that he hasn't stuck anything up his own ass. I decide that I will make him catalogue those objects between bites of dinner. Eventually I will put the spider gag on him. I want to enjoy the sight of his mouth open. Maybe the second time he comes over I will start there and work my way down. For our first time, I am exclusively interested in his ass.

I sleep well after my bath. I dream about an old building with many rooms. It looks unmistakably like my college though instead of classrooms there are cells. I walk down the halls and hear the sounds of boys fucking. The doors are oak and each has a window that is placed exactly at my eye level. I look into the first door that I come to and see Tuesday inside, hog-tied on top of Professor Alice Adams' desk. The room is populated by the men's lacrosse team. They stare at Tuesday because he is naked and beautiful. They want him but they are only students who will, at most, witness the lesson. A door next to the chalkboard opens and Alice Adams walks in. No, she struts in. She struts toward her desk in a black latex suit that forms the curves of her body into straight lines. A huge pink strap-on protrudes from her fly and Tuesday's eyes widen as she pulls a condom out of a mysterious and previously unnoticed back pocket. Alice Adams walks past the desk and Tuesday follows her with his eyes. They are the only parts of his body that can move and he stares as Alice Adams hands the condom to a redheaded boy in the front row. The boy blushes brighter than his freckles as she orders him to put his hands behind his back and put the condom on her cock using only his mouth. Once he completes the task to her satisfaction, she rewards him with a piece of chocolate to take away the taste of latex on his tongue.

Alice Adams' cock is wet with this boy's spit when she shoves it between Tuesday's lips. He grunts and gulps until he deep-throats her. The door I am peeping through opens and I find my cock in my hand ready to fuck. I spread Tuesday's ass and spit on the trembling red opening that reveals itself to me. Alice Adams and I fuck him until the three of us come, me first, Alice second, and Tuesday third. I wake up gripping the sheets. There are hours to fill until my doorbell rings.

I get some work done on my thesis: The Erotics of the Sonnet. I've been working on this project all summer and although it is only the first week of classes, I can think of no bigger turnoff than a fourteen-line poem. Maybe a haiku formed from a magnetic poetry set. The only set I've ever appreciated was the set of "dirty" magnetic poetry that I got from my dyke cousin

Jodie. There are no less than ten rectangles that read *cock*. The adjectives are impressive, from the functional, *hard,* to the more metaphorical, *effervescent.* I would like to have Tuesday compose poems with the set while sitting on a sterling silver butt plug. He'd look darling in just a white button-down shirt and a tie. He'd be pantless so I could see the plug penetrate him and run my fingers along the crevice between perineum and metal when I wanted to distract him from his task. I know this would be unfair of me but I am not attempting to be fair. I would rather dish out what a bottom needs than indulge him in what he thinks he wants. I am insidiously benevolent. My gifts are gifts. My punishments are also gifts, when viewed with the right interpretation. This is not Orwellian doublespeak, but a truth I'm sure a bright boy like Tuesday will be able to grasp.

In my house, the pleasures of the bedroom extend beyond its walls, so in preparation for Tuesday's arrival, I clean every room. I like the possibility of taking him anyplace. Every space in the house is ready. The tables and counters are clear. The floors are clean enough to eat off of. I pull a large wooden box out from under my bed and lay the gear out on a towel. I unwrap each cock, each plug, each chain, each strap, and each clip. I polish the leather with saddle soap, shine the steel, and wipe down the rest with alcohol swabs and a hint of lavender. I put everything away but a blindfold before the doorbell rings. Wanting has grown in me like a horse pounding its hooves, steam rolling out of its nostrils like the blackest aspect of fire. I conjure spurs and a whip. I tighten myself till I am calm, then I open the door and lead Tuesday in. He trembles as he kneels before me and I brush his black bangs aside to tie the blindfold. His breath is measured and I feel him sinking into where I want him, but before he goes down too deeply, I give him his safeword. I inhale. I begin.

# REMEMBERED MEN

Shane Allison

He was younger than me. He lived in a housing project. He had strawberry-blond hair with pubes to match. His ass was firm in dark blue shorts. He had kissable lips. He was an asshole all grown up. He had more foreskin than you could shake a stick at. He had a pretty big dick for someone his size. He had buck teeth. He was poor white trash who gave great head. He had an ass like a football player. He was such a nerd. He asked me to take a photo of my dick and bring it to school. He worked as an usher at a movie theatre. He liked to get fist-fucked. He sucked me off at a urinal. His brother was also gay. He wanted me to prove that I loved him by swallowing it. He fucked me sense-less. His name was Tony. He was my first. He had the worst case of dandruff. He was too damn skinny for my tastes. He had man-breasts. He had a short, fat, pretty prick. He nibbled my earlobes. He taught Spanish at the local university. His cat licked the hair grease from my head as its master rode me like a bull. His cat licked his balls from behind as his master sucked me. He came on my stomach. He parted my asscheeks. He fingered my ass with his married finger. It hurt a little, but after the initial pain, it felt pretty damn good. His dick came up to his belly button. His last name was *Cocke*. He answered the door wearing nothing but green shorts and a durag. He slapped me around and I liked it. He swallowed my cum. He made me suck his balls. He made me suck his nipples. He called me a whore. He's right. He called me a whore and I loved him even more. He stood me up. He shoved a sex toy up in me. His dick was pierced. He had a British accent. He said, "Get down there and suck it." He wore latex underwear. He never did call the next day like he said he would. He wouldn't stop calling. He started to freak me out when he came by unexpectedly. He asked, "Are you ready for the rim chair?" He was old and balding. He was fat and just right. He was a tad too sissyish for my blood. He had blushing balls in a leather cock ring. He told me I could move in if I drank his piss. He asked, "You want to be my pig boy?" He kept saying, "Let me in you." He spoke with the thickest New York accent. He lived in Jersey. He was a rough punk with tattoos. He was blond and bearded. He had three dogs. He and I drank coconut rum and talked about "Queer as Folk." His breath smelled of fish and cigarettes. He said, "I hope you're not getting drunk just to have sex with me." He was Italian and talked too much. He had hard thighs. He had filthy fingernails. He was Jewish, you know. He picked fights with me. He took the piercing out of his dick. He was much cuter with the Afro. He was HIV positive. His family had no idea. He talked dirty to me. He was called a fag by bullies and high school football players. He was happily married. He swore to me he was disease free. His wife hadn't a clue. His milk-white skin. He was moving to Europe. He told me why, but I forgot. He handcuffed me. He used the whip to take his

frustrations out on my flesh. He asked, "Are you a homosexual?" He told me to take off my pants. He held me at knife-
point. He busted us both for lewdness down by the tracks. He
was a cop undercover. He was Greek and new to the city. He
was old-fashioned. He had a white girlfriend. He was Puerto
Rican. He claimed he liked the flowers. He had soft, red fur
around his asshole. He walked me home out of the rain. His
cigarette breath on my neck. He asked as I began to finger-fuck
his ass, "Can I go to the bathroom before you do that?" He
snored and belched. He farted in my face as we sixty-nined each
other. He said, "For ten dollars I'll suck it right off the bone."
He said he wasn't a hustler, but just wanted money for something to eat. He sucked me off for two bucks. He told me he
wasn't homeless or a drug addict. He blew me right there on the
hood of his car. He worked at a gas station. His face and back
was burned. He drove an old Jaguar. He fucked me like I had a
pussy. He said, "I appreciate the cards and love letters." He said
I came on too strong. He accused me of keying his car. He was
so heavy on top of me, I couldn't breathe. His apartment had
hardwood floors. His bed with the pale-blue sheets. His roommate was asleep in the next room, but he didn't care. He told
me to keep quiet. He asked, "Do you think your roommates
would like to join in?" He drove naked through the dirt roads.
He had come three times already. He was such a pig. He asked,
"Would you like me to drink your piss now?" He called me
Shawn. He wore black shoes with buckles. His jeans and underwear pulled down around his ankles. He left his stall door open
for all to see. He told me to clean up my cum. He asked me if I
was black. He thought I was West Indian. His shirt with yellow
armpit stains. He had low-hanging balls. His dimpled bubble-
butt. His moustache pricked my lip. He left me sore for days.
His flat feet, the bony toes. His braids all in rows. His yellow

bandana. His filthy asscrack. His hairy ass in the denim chaps. His hot, Hispanic accent. His Mohawk haircut. His polished fingernails. His pierced lips around my dick. He asked me what I was into. His mouth filled with all that cum and spit. He stood me up. He avoided me in the hall. He ignored my calls. He said he didn't care about looks. His toes were pretty and pedicured. He lived in Soho. He was a geology major. He loved Steven Spielberg. He was eight years older than me. He freaked me out with his obsession for teenage boys. He worked at a bowling alley. He looked like Madonna from the *Papa Don't Preach* video. He wore a fake carnation in his hair. His head was shaved. His crotch was shaved. He was on the down low. His parents didn't know. He tinted the windows of his car so he could make out with guys in parking lots. His dirty socks thrown in the corner of the room. He had a mole on his dick. He drank too much. He was a filthy, sexist bastard. He warned me about the cops in this place. His dick with all those veins. He had all that built-up dickcheese. He liked to wear makeup. He won a glow-in-the-dark rubber in a bingo game. He was a motivational speaker who lived in the Bronx. He performed as a drag queen at a club I forget the name of. He was a pretty-eyed tranny. He dressed better than most of the women I know. He stepped out wearing a black miniskirt. He had a mullet and smelled of cheap perfume. He was bisexual. He was a drunken old queen wearing a fake fur. He was a heathen. He was a born-again Christian. He was a gay Republican. He was torn between his religion and his love for men. He was such a club kid. He was such a pretty boy. He couldn't come for doing so much coke. He paid top dollar for my soiled undies. He wanted to fuck right there in the hallway. He lived with his ailing mother. He said, "Damn you're huge." He took long whiffs of my socks. He held the poppers to my nose. He was butt-naked in the park. He fought with the drunken guy whose wallet was stolen at the Unicorn. He said, "Easy with the teeth, dude." He said, "C'mon, I'm trying to suck a dick here." He had muscles like you would not believe. He liked getting spanked. He looked like a young Jeff Daniels. He had untrustworthy eyes. He made the best vodka breezes in the West Village. His shimmering torso. He just stood there jacking off. He threw up on my dick. He gave me a soapy rag for the mess. He liked the poem I wrote. He slapped my ass with his dick. He was a Brooklyn thug. He asked if I had any weed on me. He was an Irish chef. He had to leave the club early. He said he had to go to church the next day. He had popsicle-red lips. His pink piss slit. He gave me herpes. He said, "Maybe you should start dating girls." He sucked the scat right off my dick. He cheated on his wife with me and from the looks of her, who could blame him? His name was Melvin. His dick was the first I ever sucked. He looked like Jerry Springer, but better looking. He had a dog named Byron. He was too drunk to fuck. He told me my dick was beautiful. He turned me into a size queen. He scared the hell out of us. He asked if he could join in when he caught us fucking. He said I smelled like good weed. He was this cute, Middle Eastern boy. He offered me some Jack Daniels. He left me chafed and scabbed, but I liked it. He cruised truck stops for dick. He had a baby dick. His dick was cold, but it warmed up quite nicely in my mouth. He lived for the tearooms. He liked to bite and pinch. He reminded me of all that great sex I used to have in the park. He pissed in the booths. He kicked me out and yelled, "Faggot ass!" He had hepatitis C. His cum tasted kind of Cloroxy. He said it wouldn't hurt if I just relaxed. He said, "You gotta come, man, my legs are giving out." He turned his hat backward before he started to suck me. His dick smelled bad. His name was Jonathan. He jerked off in the mayonnaise at Burger King. He wore a black shirt that said SECURITY on the back. He broke up the sex orgy. He was a rugged trucker. He said if he didn't suck a dick soon, he'd explode. He squirted and came. He wore snakeskin boots that night. He was free on Mondays and Wednesday evenings. He wanted to come on my face. He almost came in my eye. He made me come without even touching me. He asked me what I was into. He was so naïve. He said he wasn't that big. He unzipped his pants and took it out. He was right. He wasn't that big. He was really *going to town* on his dick. He said, "I love the color of your skin." He adored the taste of unclean foreskin. He said, "Now suck it, slut!" He didn't like to be watched. He said, "Go away, nigger," when I stuck my dick under his stall. He lay in white sand sunbathing in the nude. He used a dirty sock to wipe up the mess. He said, "C'mon on, man. Glide me in." He said, "You wanna butt-fuck me?" He didn't want to meet at his place due to the nosey neighbors. He fucked me in a cemetery. He bent over the bed of the truck and spread his asscheeks for me. His web name is Sexy Bear Butt. He wore a platinum blonde beehive wig. He'd only experimented with guys a few times. He and I had phone sex. He hung up as soon as I came. He said he loved me and I believed it. His name was Chris. His girlfriend found out about us. He was so big, he made me gag. He got pissed when I refused to swallow it. He laughed when I told him I had a crush on him. He shook his ass harder when I waved a dollar in his face. He drove a beat-up old Chevy. He came all over my maroon sweater. He drove a green Camaro. He threw my love letters away. He patted me on the head when I swallowed his cum. His breath was a mixture of peppermint and fish. He used to be a woman. He took me to Woodstock for the weekend. He had one ball, but a big, thick dick. He was my sugar daddy. He loved to get gangbanged. He tied me up. He gagged me with his stinking underwear. He was all the rage at the bathhouses. He believed in monogamy. He was a nelly bottom. He liked it rough. He sucked us both off. He said it felt good when his wife used a dildo. He found the Polaroids of my dick in a folder. He was such a sissy slut. He was a teddy bear bottom. He told me that my dick was a perfect fit. He'd always fantasized about what sex would be like with a black guy. He tugged my balls too hard. He liked how gentle I was. He wasn't into white guys. He cheated on his wife. His greasy anal plugs. He wore panties under his jeans. His girlfriend had no idea. He cock blocked me from the other boys. He said, "I keep my ass clean and love to get eaten." He preferred to rim a dirty asshole. He sucked me off on a stack of corn in the storage room where we used to be movie ushers. He had that one gold tooth in the front. He said, "You shot a big load." He confessed that his accent was fake and that he was really from Georgia. He struggled to stuff his dick in me all night long, but never got it in. He said I was tight. He got fucked by some guy he didn't know. He liked it bareback. He wanted me to come in his ass. He said, "Don't nut in my mouth." He drank my cum like it was beer. He kept saying, "Fuck me like I fuck my wife." He couldn't give head for shit to be such a slut. His ass smelled like Irish Spring. He ate me out for countless hours. He was able to fit two dicks up his ass at once. He said, "Let me see those titties." He wanted to sniff my feet while he jacked off. He left an imprint of his asscheeks on the dashboard of my truck. He said, "Too sweaty, dude, too sweaty." (Meaning my butt.) He was a famous poet. He said my underwear wasn't ripe enough. He yelled, "Fuck my white ass!" He bled a bit. His dick was wet and nasty, but I sucked him anyway. He shot a load on my painter pants. He didn't want his wife to know. He asked me if I had a place. He wore black boxers with red Playboy bunnies on them. He wore a flannel shirt with the sleeves cut off. He said, "I'll cut your fucking throat." He was a fine piece of Mexican ass. He was such a cock tease. He wore a Silence=Death T-shirt. His wife seemed nice. He smelled like baby powder down there. He said, "Hold on to me while I come." He said to me, as I blew him, "I knew I would get some action tonight if I came here." He doesn't have the time for me now that his girlfriend has moved in. He likes to call me a *nigger* while I suck him off. He wants white, young dick only. His shaved balls. He has a black mouth for a white cock. He took a rubber out of the glove compartment. He was a hot, white male seeking same. He took his clothes off. His bare ass behind the bar. He stuck his dick under my stall. His wife wasn't home so my timing was perfect. He asked, "You didn't come in my ass did you?" He said that Jason Bartlett is a flaming faggot. (Whoever the hell Jason Bartlett is.) He drank too much. His name was Ronny. He loved to wear diapers and blue bonnets. He could fit a Ping-Pong ball up that ass. He put his shirt back on when I walked into the office. His big, Cuban dick. He videotaped us having sex. He was a virgin.

# THE PANCAKE CIRCUS

Trebor Healey

Clown Daddy bused dishes at the Pancake Circus, a tacky breakfast joint on Broadway in Sacramento. I only went there when I was depressed and, in my half-baked noncommittal self-destruction, craving food that would kill me if I ingested enough of it. I wanted a steamy stack of buttermilk pancakes with that whipped butter they use that melts slowly and thoroughly, sort of like my psyche does when it's heading south. (It does not have the same effect on your arteries, however, which slowly harden like dog shit in the sun.) And I wanted that diabetes-inducing syrup, of course. Two or three shots of it—lethal as sour mash—surreptitious, sticky and sweet as it vanishes into the spongy cake, absorbed like a criminal into the social fabric.

Clown Daddy began as a tattoo of a tiger jumping through a ring of fire—a tiger with a pacifier in his mouth. A tiger caged in a mess of plump blue veins—veins like the roots that buckle sidewalks. Straining as they held the pot poised over my cup;

straining like my throat suddenly was; like my cock caged in my drawers.

"Coffee?" It was Josh Hartnett's voice.

In an effort to compose myself, I drew a breath and followed those veins up that forearm, down through the dimple of its elbow and up across the creamy white bicep, firm and round as a young athlete's buttcheek, before the blood-swollen tubes vanished into his white polyester shirt, re-appearing at the neck and passing the Adam's apple, which was nothing less than a mushroom head pushing boy-boisterously out of his neck-skin like a go-go dancer in Tommies. *God have mercy,* my soul muttered, as my eyes, having lost his veins somewhere under his chin (and damn, what a beautiful charcoal-shadowed chin), proceeded with anticipation up his clean-shaven cheek, savoring the pheromonal (and I mean "moan"-al) beauty of him, dead set for his eyes like a junkie tightening the belt. And bingo, like apples and oranges lining up in a slot—oh my god, I won!

I'm a homo and you know where I'd look for the coins. I felt my sphincter dilate, and my buttcheeks were suddenly like open-cupped palms, holding themselves out to him.

I came in my pants. And then, a bit unnerved to say the least, cleared my throat. I'm not sure I would have been able to even answer him if I hadn't relieved the pressure somewhere. Fortunately, God had mercy after all.

I whimpered, "Yes, please." I couldn't even look at him, so I watched the cup as he filled it to the top, and then some. It crested the brim and ran down onto the saucer—and then I watched the pot move away, off to the next table.

Jesus H. go-go-dancing Christ. My drawers were soaked and cooling. I felt like a kid who'd wet his pants. This had happened to me only once before, in junior high, when Greg Vandersee had stretched, lifting up his arms and revealing a divine cunt of underarm hair that made me lurch forward as my cock emptied its boy-fresh copious fluids into my little BVDs.

Fortunately, Clown Daddy was a busboy and not my waiter. I could handle *yes* and *no,* but *the buttermilk stack, with sausage and one egg over easy* wouldn't have been pretty—or perhaps even possible.

"Hi, I'm Edna. What'll you have?" She smiled.

*A bed, some lube, and an hour with your busboy* would have been the honest answer. *Or a fresh pair of undergarments.* But this wasn't about honesty, this was about self-destruction. Wasn't it? I ordered the low-cholesterol eggbeaters in a vegetable omelet with whole wheat toast. Say what you will—lust leads to healthy choices. Doesn't it?

What I hadn't realized as I sat back gloating, my penis clammy in my damp, semen-soaked briefs, was that when I'd looked in Clown Daddy's eyes my days as a law-abiding citizen had abruptly ended. Choices? Choices had nothing to do with it.

But ignorance is bliss. While it lasts. And while it lasted, my head wobbled like one of those big-headed spring-loaded dolls that resemble Nancy Reagan, swinging this way and that, watching for him, rolling up and down and around like an amusement park ride, taking in the Pancake Circus as I did so, its paint-by-number clowns adorning the walls, its circus tent decor, its uncanny ambience of a sick crime waiting to happen.

I watched him move about while my fly tightened like a glove over a fist. A wet fist, sticky and greedy for whatever it had just crushed to sticky pulp. My mind played the sideshow song as I imagined Clown Daddy behind the curtain, Edna up front barking for him: "Step right up, see the man who makes you cum in your drawers!"

I gulped the coffee down, which drew him back to my table like a shark to wet, red, bleeding bait.

He didn't look at me until I thanked him, and then it was just a shy, straightboy grin. God, but his features were sharp, angled, and clean. His dark, deep-set eyes, the long lashes, the wide mouth with its full lips, the arresting pale blue-white of his skin and the night-black hair—that goddamn shadowed chin. And his eyes: dark as crude oil, raw out of the ground. He was undeniably, painfully handsome. Prozac handsome because he cheered me up. Wellbutrin handsome because one saw one's sadness disappear like a wisp of smoke—and those pesky sexual side effects? Gone. Every woman in the place blushed when he cleared their plates. I probably wasn't the only one stuck to the vinyl seat in my booth. Thank God my cock has no voice or it would have been barking like a dog.

But I felt the letdown all the same. He's probably straight. Though he ignored the blushing dames. He seemed even a little annoyed by their attention. But we knew who each other were, the girls and I. I eyed them and they me. Did I look as greedy as them? Like there was one cabbage patch doll left and they'd kill to wrest it from whatever fellow shopper had his or her eye on it. Fact was, we all had holes we wanted his cock in. Simple as that. It was like there was one tree left in the world and the ditches yelped like graves to be the chosen one.

I gulped my food like a scat queen falling off the wagon. Delirious, my diaper soiled, I paid my check and left, one glance over the shoulder to see him bend to pick up a fallen fork. Damn, Clown Daddy had a butt like a stallion. My dog leapt, knocking over the milk dish again. Jesus H. cock-hungry Christ. I lurched out the door as my piss slit opened like a flume on a dam.

Clown Daddy sent me home in a frenzy, is what he did.

I rushed home, needing to get naked. Onto my back on my bed, my legs kicking like an upended insect as I pulled like a madman, again and again, on my slot handle, hitting jackpot after jackpot until my bed was plain lousy with change.

From then on, he filled my nights and days like a cup, brimming over.

I went for more pancakes two days later, but he wasn't there. On the third day, he was, with a beautiful zit on his cheek. Clown Daddy looked right through me when he recognized me, and then he pulled himself back out.

I lurched. Shit—I came again.

"Coffee?"

"Uh, yeah," I half-coughed.

"Cream?"

I nodded. The greed. My shorts were already full of it.

"Sugar?" He's talkative today.

I regained my composure. "No sugar—sugar's for kids," I answered flirtatiously.

I don't know why I said it. I had to say something. I wanted to hold him there, even if for only a few seconds.

He smiled the brightest smile, and walked away.

My head swiveled. What was that? Had he flirted back?

While I waited for my waitress, I read the ads urethaned into the tabletop: vacuum repair, van conversions, derogatory credit, body shops, auto detailing, furniture, appliances, and bail bonds. The clues were everywhere. It occurred to me then that he was the only white busboy in the place. The rest were illegal Latin guys who didn't have a choice. What would a citizen take a job like this for? Maybe he was Rumanian or something. But he had no accent. What could he be making?—four, five bucks an hour? Hell, his looks alone could get him ten doing nothing for the right boss. He could hustle at two hundred an hour, do porn for a few thousand a feature; he could wait tables and fuck up and they'd still forgive him because the doyennes of Sacramento would return for the way he made them feel against their seat cushions. *What* was he doing here?

Who *cares*. Just let me fuck him. Shoot first, ask questions later.

He was as aloof as ever when he came back with the coffee. Three cups later, I asked for sugar. He smiled again. "Sugar's for kids. You like kids?"

"Sure, kids are all right."

He nodded and raised his brows with just a hint of a grin as he said, sort of stoned-like, "Kids are all right." And he walked away.

Go figure. I scribbled my phone number on the coffee coaster, with a little cartoon kid, waving.

And he called. But he never left his name.

"This is the guy who likes kids, down at the Circus. I can't leave a number, but meet me at the Circus at three Wednesday."

I jacked off at 2:30, not wanting to repeat my little Pancake Circus habitual jackpot when I sidled up to shake his hand. My knees might buckle, and then what? Would I hold onto his hand and pull him down with me? Would I beg him to clean up my shorts with his tongue? Would he do it?

I needed to get hold of myself. I turned the key in the deadbolt as I left the house. I pushed the key in hard, my mouth agape. In and out went the key. I reached for the knob. Good god, I've lost it.

I saw him from two blocks away. He sat on the low wall of the planter that had endured, neglected and falling to pieces with its ratty bushes and weeds, between the sidewalk and the parking lot.

He wore black boots, Levis, and a camouflage winter coat. Not a promising fashion statement for what I had in mind.

He nodded when he saw me coming, but ignored my hand when I put it out to shake. He just said, "What's up?" And then, without waiting for an answer, added, "There's a playground about five blocks from here."

"What?"

"Come on, I'll show you."

I feigned having a clue, but I really didn't have one until it occurred to me he might be suggesting a place to have sex—some doorway maybe, or a clump of trees out of view that school-yards were notorious for. But it was three P.M., school would still be in session.

I could see the schoolyard fence from a couple blocks away as we approached. Stepping off a curb, he abruptly grabbed my arm by the bicep, and my cock leapt like a Jack Russell terrier.

"Stop here," he stated flatly.

I looked at him inquisitively, at a loss. He dropped his gaze and I followed it as, with his left hand firmly in his pocket, he lifted his pant leg slowly to reveal a plastic contraption surrounding his ankle. A small green light pulsed intermittently. He studied it, then, backing up three feet, got it to stop pulsing and simply glow a constant green.

"This is as far as I can go," he stated, matter-of-factly.

It took me a minute to realize he was under house arrest. What does it mean? I didn't know anything about law enforce-ment. Drunk driving? It must be some kind of probation. He's probably a rapist or a killer, a thief or a drug dealer. Nah, too cute to rape. But if he's fucked up enough, what would that matter? Too smart to kill. Thieves are a dime a dozen and I'm only carrying twenty bucks. Drug-dealing? Humbug. So what. But none of these possibilities were in any way convincing. He was just too sexy to fit any criminal stereotype, which shows you what a dumbfuck I was.

I may have misread him, but I wasn't completely foolish. Not completely. I knew he was a criminal, so I figured I'd need to find out about the ankle bracelet before taking him home. Just in case he was going to murder me or steal my stereo. The logic of queers. On top of all that, I assumed he'd tell me the truth, which was preposterous—except that he did. More or less.

He retired to a sloping lawn in front of a house on the corner, offering, "This will be fine." I was getting more and more confused. Sex right here?

Within minutes, we heard them: the cacophony of tykes, who were now streaming down the street in gaggles. They reached the far corner, stopped, looked both ways, and then proceeded across. Group after group of them: little Koreans and Viets with rolling book bags, Mexican kids burdened by overstuffed backpacks, white kids on skateboards, little black kids strutting.

"Aren't they beautiful?" he said.

"Sure they are," I concurred. "Kids are like flowers."

"Flowers?" He looked at me like I was stupid.

"You know, those colorful things? New life? All that?" He wasn't buying my poetry.

"I mean beautiful like meat," and he ran his tongue lasciviously across his full upper lip as it occurred to me, amidst my throbbing erection, that he was a pedophile. My cock was like a poised spear now, but not because of what he'd just confessed about his sexual orientation—it was his tongue and what it had just performed. Take me, you beast. I must confess, the moral repugnance was not the first thought that entered my mind, nor the second. The tongue being the first, what followed was my sudden disappointment that not only was I possibly the wrong gender, but I was most definitely not the right age. I hadn't a chance. My cock still reached for him, fighting against the

binding of my jeans—not to mention the limits of his orientation—like a child having a tantrum, refusing to let go of a cher-
ished teddy bear. But I felt the sweat on my asshole cool.

He lay back, a sprig of grass in his teeth, smiling at the kids—a
pedophile cad. They smiled back. Jesus Wayne Gacy, we were
cruising!

I tried to get a foothold. "Uh, would you like to go grab a
coffee?"

"Nah, I'm happy right here."

I said nothing more, paralyzed with ineptitude. We sat there
for just fifteen minutes, until the herd had passed.

"Damn, I gotta jack off. Come on."

Speaking of come-ons—was this one? I'm not sure I was
interested anymore, but of course my cock still was, throbbing
like a felon in chains. I followed.

Back to Broadway, to an ugly stucco motel-looking apartment
building streaked with rusty drain runoff, its windows curtained
and unwelcoming. Clown Daddy said nothing. He simply keyed
the lock, and I followed him into one of the saddest apartments
I'd ever seen. A mattress lay in the middle of the living room,
with a single twisted blanket on it. There was an alarm clock on
the floor, and in the kitchen, fast food trash in the sink.

The toilet was foul and ringed with dark grime. There were
no pictures, no kitchen utensils, plates, or cups, no toaster, no
coffee maker, no books, no phone. Other than the bed and the
roof and plumbing, there was but one thing that made the place
habitable at all: a TV with a VCR.

He pulled a videocassette out of the back lining of his camouflage hunting jacket and placed it in the VCR. He sat down on
the bed, suddenly eager and animated. "I just got this from a
dude I met. It better be good; it cost me thirty bucks." There

were no credits, no title, not even sound. There were a lot of kids though, doing things that got people put away.

"I think I better go," I muttered, when all at once, with his elbows now supporting him on the bed, he leaned back and yanked his jeans down, revealing an enormous marbled manhood that slapped back across his taut belly like a call to prayer. His eyes fixed on the TV, never even acknowledging his handsome cock as he grabbed it full-fisted. *Jesus God,* I muttered to myself, staring at one of the most stunning penises I'd ever seen: nine inches, wired like the backside of a computer with mouth-watering veinage, and nested in the blackest of hair, which right now was casting deep forested shadows as it worked its way under his well-stocked jumbo-sized scrotum. I never had a choice. It was in my mouth before I made any decisions or even considered whether he wanted it there. He didn't protest, bucking his hips and driving into my whimpering mouth as he glared at the TV set. I shot in my pants without so much as touching myself, just moments before my throat filled like a cream pastry, hot gobs of his God-juice leaking from the crust.

I tongued it clean before he quickly grabbed it like a hammer, or anything else I could have been borrowing, to put it away. He didn't even look at me as he hopped to his feet, yanking up his jeans in one fluid motion. It wasn't fear of intimacy like I'd seen with other guys. He was simply done, and more or less emotionless—in his own world. God knows what he'd been thinking as he bucked his manly juices into my craving body, which for him had become just one big hole to propel his antisocial lusts into. I can't call it my mouth; it was just what was available. I'd have torn my skin back like curtains if it were possible and let him drill through whatever part of me got him off.

"That tape sucked," he casually related. I was still sitting on the bed, stunned, not knowing what to do, licking the remnants of his now-cooling semen off my chapped lips. "I gotta go to work," he informed me, pulling the videocassette out and handing it to me, without making eye contact.

"Uh, I don't want this," I said as my hand opened to accept it.

"No? Don't you like kids?"

"Uh, I think you know what I like."

He said nothing. Then: "Keep it for me 'til next time." And he grinned.

"Next time?" I was in a daze, but hope springs eternal.

"Yeah, next time I see you." I lit up even though I was consumed with dread from what, other than the amazing cock action, was a profoundly depressing social interaction.

"I'll just leave it here," I said, balking.

"No can do, guy. I'm on probation. Can't have that here. Keep it for me."

"Uh, yeah, sure, 'til next time."

I didn't think myself an accomplice as I walked home. What did I know about such legal machinations? I only knew I was no longer depressed and had just had one of life's peak experiences. Had his cock literally trounced thousands of years of science that had eventually developed selective serotonin reuptake inhibitors? Imagine the clinical trials. I'd seen a lot of cocks, a lot of naked men, like any fag. But Jesus H. Priapus Satyriasis, I had never seen such a beautiful manifestation of the male organ anywhere—in print, on film, in my bed, even in my fantasy life, which was no slacker when it came to cock. I imagined what it must have been like for explorers coming upon Yosemite, Victoria Falls, the Grand Canyon. Unimaginable and sublime beauty. I leaned against a wall at one point on the walk home, needing to catch my breath, my cock once again tenting my jeans. The fact of the matter was: I was strung out on his cock. And I didn't even have a phone number.

No matter. He called, thank god. It was either that or I was in for a lot of pancakes.

"I got some more tapes. Wanna come over and check them out?"

I didn't hear any of it but the come over part. "When?"

"Now."

"I'm on my way."

The door was cracked when I arrived. When I opened it to step in, I lost my breath. Splayed across the bed was Clown Daddy, his substantial manhood like the clock tower at some university—everything converged toward it.

"Oh baby," was all I could think to say, which was oddly appropriate considering what was happening on the VCR where his gaze was fixed. My brows furrowed. Good god, they can't be more than three.

"Come to poppa," he said with a fatherly grin.

I was like a panting puppy with the promise of a walk. He held the leash. I leapt and was sucking on his teat like a hungry lamb before you could say baahhh, drooling and lapping up and down the hard shaft, savoring the throbbing gristle of his veins, weeping at the sweet softness of the massive velvety helmet. I was aware of what felt like a tear rolling down my inner thigh. My asshole was sweating like a day laborer short on rent: more baskets, more peaches.

I knew I needed to strip but balked at taking a time-out for fear he'd lose interest or lose control. I hopped up and stripped quickly. He didn't even notice, his eyes locked on the romper room shenanigans stage left like a baby enthralled with a mobile.

I knew all I had to do was get into position, and in no time was on my knees, facing the TV, blocking Clown Daddy's view. He didn't miss a beat as he hopped up on his knees and grabbed my waist, answering my plea for "Lube, Clown

Daddy, lube," with a hawk into his palm.

I opened like sunrise, pulled him into me more than he plunged. I heard him as he vanished into my sleeve: "Uuuuuuuuuuuuuuuhhh." And I matched him like a chorus: "Aaaaaaaaaaaaahhhhhh." I dropped my face into the mattress as he pounded me, knowing I'd be unable to maintain any balance with my arms, which not only were shaking with excitement, but were seriously challenged considering the slams he was delivering and the fact that my body's focus was pretty much solely directed at the contractions of my rectum as it greedily grabbed at what can only be described as the bread of life. A baguette of it, no less.

He sent me onto the floor by thrust ten or so, and then he emitted an enormous Josh Hartnett "FUUUUck," as my asshole filled with his ambrosia.

He pulled out with a *pop* and wiped his cock with the blanket and fell backward onto his back. "That's a great age," he wistfully concluded, staring at the ceiling.

I felt a momentary sinking feeling as I looked at the video monitor, realizing all at once the makeover I would need if I was to hold onto Clown Daddy past the duration of his probation.

"I gotta go to work," he stated. I nodded; I knew the protocol. He popped out the tape and handed it to me. I staggered down the walkway of that shitty apartment building past dried-out cactuses in pots and a pair of roller skates—good God, did his or her parents know who was living next door? What about Megan's Law? I was lost in a strange milieu of overarching lust, revulsion, horror, responsibility, and that unique postfuck feeling of *that was great; everything's gonna be just fine.*

At home, I fumbled through my bathroom drawers for the Flowbee and set to work shaving my body clean of hair. While my mind remained a stew of anxiety, and I winced at the razor nicks I was inflicting on my balls, I reveled in how I was going to finally incite his lust as he had mine.

Next, I got out my sewing machine and set to work on a new wardrobe: a sailor suit, a Boy Scout uniform, a large diaper, Teletubbie briefs.

I put on the briefs and sailor suit, looked at myself in the mirror. Ridiculous. *Don't be so negative,* I self-talked back. I did a striptease, attempting to be convincing. I worked on my little-boy shy look. But when I finally dropped my trousers and gazed at my hairless cock, I was sorely dismayed. I had a big dick, huge really, and the shaving had only made it look bigger. How am I gonna convince Clown Daddy I'm a child with this thing? How many grade-schoolers are packing eight inches? Then there was my chest and arms. I worked out, for God's sake; I was a mess of secondary sex characteristics. I needed to gain fifty pounds, maybe take some hormones. *One step at a time,* I calmed myself.

I'd done what I could and I wanted to see him, to show him how I'd be whatever he wanted me to be. I don't think at that time I was considering saving him and reforming him. I just wanted to please him, make of myself a gift. Woo him.

Chocolate. I bought a box of Le Petite Ecoliers and went for pancakes. He smiled big when he saw me. The hostess looked askance. The crowd wondered. It occurred to me I was exposing him. I blushed red as a swollen cockhead. I left as quickly as I'd come, racing back up the street. Whatever happened, I didn't want to hurt Clown Daddy. Goodness no, I was interested in his pleasure.

There was a message on the machine when I got home: "Nice suit, hee, hee. Eight P.M. Wear it." Click.

* * *

The shirt never came off, as Clown Daddy's maleness hovered over me and he ominously climbed up on top of me, his lead pipe of a cock bobbing like a tank gun, my legs held behind my ears like the spring-loaded pogo stick I would soon be playing the part of as he bounced me off the mattress.

"You look fucking great," he smiled, and he kissed me this time, full, his tongue like a tapeworm, bent on my intestines, determined to reach all the way down to where his cock was reaching from the other end to meet it in a hot sticky mess of saliva and semen.

"Daddy, daddy, daddy," I yelped. We growled, we lost ourselves and rode our dicks like runaway horses. His final thrusts were so divine, my hands digging into his firm white buttcheeks like talons holding their kill. He split me like a piece of wood and my cum hit his chest so hard it bounced and splattered like blood would if the axe of his cock had buried itself in my forehead.

I'd brought the diaper in my backpack.

"Daddy...please...diaper me."

He guffawed, and then with an eagerness I'd never seen, yelped, "Yeeeeaaah!"

He diapered me. Patted my ass. Told me to pack up and get out.

My god, I'd done it. I'd seduced Clown Daddy.

He didn't kiss me good-bye, of course, or invite me to brunch. But I walked away without a videocassette this time. Progress.

I guess that's when it occurred to me I could save him. And maybe not only him. Maybe I'd just found the treatment for pedophilia. God knows, no one seemed to give a damn about these people. The last sexual minority. I could rehabilitate them all. My shaved asshole, a rehab center.

That's when I saw the squad car. Parked in front of my house. Next to the undercover white Crown Royal. Three men in dark suits. It was *The Matrix* and I was Neo, standing on a street corner in a sailor suit, my hips bulging from the diaper that swaddled my manhood.

I knew what they'd found. I knew my chances. I ran. It wasn't much of a chase. I had nowhere to go. All I had was a shot at making it back to Broadway where the great voting public could witness four cops tackling a child—a rather large child, to be sure—in a sailor suit.

I felt the tug as one of them got hold of the back of my shirt just as I reached the intersection of 23rd and Broadway. I screamed as high-piercing a preadolescent scream as I could muster.

I was interrogated at length. I assumed they had Clown Daddy somewhere. How else would they have nabbed me? I drank coffee, got knocked around, but through it all I endured by dreaming of meeting Clown Daddy—when I was finally convicted—in some filthy prison cell where we could pursue our love affair in peace—me trading cigarettes and gum for razors to keep my cock and balls soft as a baby's behind for my Clown Daddy and his meat-Eucharist, truly a transubstantiation of all the misery around us into an Elysian Field of bliss.

"Where did you get the tapes?"

I refused to tell. "I found them."

"Where?"

I had to place them as far away from Clown Daddy as possible. "In a trashcan in Vacaville."

"What were you doing going through trash in Vacaville?"

"Someone on the Internet told me he'd put them there." I was indicting myself. I thought I was saving Clown Daddy. If I had to lie, even to the point of destroying my own future, I'd do it for Clown Daddy—blinded by love, or myopia for his cock. Same difference. And to think I didn't even know the details of his crime. We'd never discussed it. I didn't want to know.

"Who?" The cop demanded, but in a boring, annoying, nonsexual way. Why couldn't Clown Daddy be my interrogator?

"It was one of those throwaway names."

"What was it?"

"Bob."

"Goddammit! Bob who?"

"Bob1 at aol-dot-com."

*Whack!* And he backhanded me across the face.

They threatened me with a stiff sentence if I didn't give them something. I only considered that their sentence could never be as stiff as Clown Daddy's meaty member, so I was unimpressed by their threats.

They gave me five years.

Clown Daddy did not appear in my cellblock, though I looked and waited and pined. It had been explained in my trial that the videos found in my home had been coded with a tracking device, leading the authorities to my house. Not unlike an ankle bracelet such as Clown Daddy wore. It had even been suggested that Clown Daddy was a narc, or had used me as a patsy. The judge put a stop to those conjectures, admonishing the defense: "Whoever gave him the pornography is not on trial today. Another day. Right now, we're trying this man." And he pointed at me like Clown Daddy's member used to do.

Clown Daddy never appeared. Only Vernon. He was my cellmate, and, as a skinny white fag, he informed me I'd be wise to do his bidding. I've done it, though he lacks both Clown Daddy's girth and length, not to mention all the other characteristics that gods wield over man.

Ah, but the gods are kind for they have blest us with imagination. And so when Vernon slicks his member with Crisco I steal from the commissary and mercilessly impales me, I close my eyes and see a circus tent, and the circus music begins, and all the clowns drop their baggy pants, and then the tigers and lions turn, lifting their tails, and the dwarves and ape men offer up their tight behinds, hands firmly gripped to their ankles—and the crowd cheers, and then goes AAAHHH as Clown Daddy in all his naked huge-dicked grinning Josh Hartnett–throated glory comes swinging through on the trapeze spraying his jism all over the clowns and animals, dwarves and freaks, and the whole damn crowd, who bathe in it as in the blessed waters of Lourdes.

And Vernon is proud. He thinks he's made that mess all over my chest and belly. Let him think it. The truth is hardly important at this point. I'm an innocent man doing time for kiddie porn, the police are fools, Vernon's a chump, and my asshole's just a 7-Eleven that he holds up every Saturday night. As for the cash, I hand it right over. In fact, I leave the register open. No way to run a business. But I, unlike Vernon, am not proud. For I have seen God.

I spend all my time with him. Vernon that is, not God. We even eat pancakes together. I stuff my face. I'm fattening up for Clown Daddy, while Vernon goes on and on with his theories.

"The earth is a plate," he tells me. "Mankind sat down and is eating. When he's through, it'll be over."

"Where are we now?" I ask, bored.

"Somewhere deep in the mashed potatoes; maybe halfway through."

"Are you gay, Vernon?" I like to get a rise out of him.

"Not at all," he explains. He tells me men are pigs, and

this is why you can't call him a faggot. Vernon says if it were legal most men he knew (and he knew a certain kind, though he always meant every man) would fuck everything in sight, and what's more, they'd never let their sex partners survive to betray them (as they always will, by his reckoning—something to remember when I get out of here). Therefore, he's of the opinion that men "would drill holes in their sex partner's skulls if they could, and fuck their brains out. They'd drill holes in backs and arms, thighs, through the bottom of feet, right through the front of 'em, core the motherfuckers like apples," he says drolly, "leave them like the dough after all the cookies have been cut out of it. But the screaming would be annoying, so you'd do the brain first."

"Do you like the circus, Vernon?"

He shrugs his shoulders. "I don't like those clowns. Creepy."

"I knew a clown once."

"Shut up and eat."

I pour more syrup on my pancakes and watch it vanish, watch it run away and join the circus.

# ORANGE

Lee Houck

Step one: Pick a moment in your life. Press your finger down onto it, holding it like you would the first loop in a square knot. Step two: Find a moment that represents where you are now, something separate, current and different, and touch another finger to that, too. Step three: Measure the distance from one to the other—in lovers lost, furniture stolen from street corners, estimated electric bills paid, early morning phone solicitations, car accidents you witnessed. Band-Aids on fingers. Step four: Figure out how the hell you got here now from where you were then.

Sometimes the first moment I choose is my cheesy orange fingertips in the propped-open back end of a station wagon parked on the tire-tracked sand of a crowded Florida beach. I must have been three years old. I don't remember it, but I have seen the photograph of me sitting there—blue and yellow tub of Cheese Balls between my diapered legs, hand stuck inside. Blond hair, just like now. When you look at pictures of yourself doing things that you don't remember, the image freezes and becomes part of your history, even though it seems invented. A memory that forms who you are without you knowing it. Like genes, unconscious but familiar.

Sometimes the moment is foamy orange Circus Peanuts melting on the dashboard of a pickup truck. We were driving there without any place to be, or any place in mind to end up in. He bought a Mountain Dew because it was my favorite. I should tell you about the way his hands moved when he talked. The way words seemed to burst out of his fingers. The urgency, the way he made even garbage seem like quantum physics. But it all gets screwed around in my brain. Memory serves only to fuck things up. And photographs can lie to you, because if you have a picture of someone, and he goes away, dies or disappears, the photo becomes the only thing you remember about him.

How did this start?

Shredded carrots at a salad bar, on some school trip in a shopping mall?

A completely mediocre, but still your favorite, orange-tinted album cover?

The smooth spine of an unread paperback book?

Other times, like this time right now, right here in this guy's bedroom, it's greasy orange cleanup wipes, the kind that he rubbed up and down his arms before climbing up behind me. "Do you like to get fucked?" he says.

A giant of a man, six foot plus something. Huge, but not alien-looking, still handsome, still attractive. A tiny line of mustache. He's bulky like a sack of flour, his body dense, smooth like rising dough. Forearms thick as a coffee can, covered in what I guess is car grease or engine grime, a shiny ultraviolet glimmer. Smells like steel. Skin brown underneath.

His lips are drawn on so beautifully that I can't help but

look right into his mouth when he's talking, and not into his eyes. He kisses my hand.

He's holding a white plastic tub. Tearing off the lid, he pulls out a strip of creamy orange-colored cheesecloth. A powerful knock-your-ass-on-the-floor kind of scent. The most fake, plastic, outer space, movie-smelling orange. Good though. The orange-powered grease cutter is pasted into the spaces of the cheesecloth. He rubs his hands, detailing the knuckles, the cuticles. And the smell of it hangs around through the entire act. Through the rough fingers, unclipped nails tugging at my warm knot of skin, before he's climbing up behind me.

Once again, I end up on my stomach. And I realize that when he reaches his arm around my face, around my neck, and grabs on to my shoulder with his hand—starting to really fuck me hard—that I'd better get fucking control of myself. I start to flatten out. In my head, I mean. I start finding that preaware, rocklike place where I can concentrate. I go to the place where everything is flat. I'm inhaling, looking for that sugary ashy smell, and suddenly, uncontrollably, my brain begins its hyperjourney back to twelve years old. Memories hijack my neurons. Memories of taste, of touch, of fake orange, and when I place my mouth on this guy's arm, it all becomes clear. I'm no longer in this place, in this bedroom. My head, my brain, myself, it's all somewhere entirely different.

We're pushing our bikes up this giant hill, and the bugs are swarming around our heads. Hot Southern summer, with salty beads of sweat around our brows and upper lips. Slapping our necks with our dusty hands, smashing black gnats. Sometimes one will fly into your mouth. But we don't care when they do. And when we get to the top of the hill we find a beat-up old cassette tape, cracked open and spilling its threads of sound onto the pavement. And we unwind the tape, a huge, hundred-foot string. And we snap it in half at the middle, tying the pieces onto the seats of our bikes, and ride back down the hill, watching the glittering of who knows what on cassette flowing behind us like a tail, like a stretched-out wish, like a thin brown destiny.

We're driving a beat-up white car through a rainstorm at three o'clock in the morning in the middle of Mississippi—or maybe we'd made it to Alabama without seeing the sign, or maybe we were still in Louisiana. And the rain is coming down so hard that we can't see the street in front of us. And we're both thinking *tornado warning for upper and lower Alabama*, but we don't say it out loud. So for three hours we travel what adds up to be forty-two miles on the low-shoulder freeway. We pass a few cars parked on the side, determined to wait it out. And in those three hours; the loud, wind-shaken hours; we don't speak. I squint, my eyes low along the top of the dash, and he drives, tapping the gas pedal, not braking, easing on, rolling back toward home. Then, crossing the state line, we see the brightness of the morning. I look over at him, he stares ahead.

And when he loosens his grip around my neck, around my head, when my mouth breaks free from the inside of his elbow, the awfulness of the present returns. This guy, this orange-smelling grease monkey, barks in my ear about how he wants to tie me up. Haven't I heard all this before? You would think it was tattooed across my forehead: TIE ME UP, TIE ME UP!

He knots my hands to the bed frame, rope made of something natural, cotton I think. Blocks my legs apart with a short two-by-four. So I'm spread-eagle on this bed, on my stomach, of course, and the knots rub raw places into my wrists. And I know that if I didn't tug so much on the rope, then it wouldn't rub so much. But he asks me to struggle a little, and I don't know how much is a little. So I do it until he starts going, "Yeah, yeah."

We used to take drives out to nowhere on weeknights. He'd smoke and we'd put a mix tape on and take turns talking. About what we wanted to do when we grew up, even though we were sixteen and didn't know what we wanted to do when we grew up. And didn't really care. And what we wanted to do would change every few miles, every few minutes. And we were grown up already. We'd pass rusted farm machinery, crumbling frames jutting out of the browning grass, leaping out of the dirt. Out near the deserted factory that you'd ride past if you went far enough. He'd take pictures of me in front of it. He wouldn't let me take pictures of him, he said he didn't like having his picture taken. I wouldn't smile because I knew what we were doing was serious. And he knew it was serious. And so he didn't ask me to smile. We didn't have to pretend. It was too hard to pretend. And mostly it still is.

We were fifteen and hiking up the part of the trail that was marked Do Not Enter. Because the best parts of the mountain were marked Do Not Enter. We'd stand at the tip of the rock, where the trail went shooting straight out into the air, over the waterfall, the canopy. The place where red-tailed hawks spiraled in circles, heavy wings lifted by the fast and beautiful air. The place where he put his arm on my shoulder. And we stood quiet. I could hear the thumping of my heartbeat in my ears, in my chest, in the tingling pulsing pressure of my fingertips. Some nights we slept outside in heavy nylon sacks, drowning in the half-light of the moon. Some nights we climbed trees, or burned pine-needle shapes in the road. Picked blueberries and ate them in the dark.

And I see him pull open the bedside table drawer, noticing the grease mark he missed on the back of his elbow. The orange air is thick and clammy around my head, stuck inside my nose, taking my olfactory canals hostage. He opens the drawer, rustles through the dog-eared *TV Guide*, the (what is that, a compact?) the Q-Tips and wadded up tissues. He pulls out a syringe. And the needle goes down into the side of my arm, a warm yellow energy flushing out my veins. If pain and happiness were mixed together and held in liquid suspension, that'd be almost what it felt like. And here's where everything comes slamming back into me, tearing open the little fear pockets in my head. I jerk hard on my wrists and there's nothing. No response. Like waking up too fast and you fall down. Only here the falling feels so fucking good. All of a sudden, falling without impact. So I slam my face back into the pillow, like a fool trying to reenter a dream. Saying softly to myself "Come on, come on, come on."

And he pushes the needle (a different needle?) down into my arm again.

And like two trains colliding, *all 142 passengers are presumed dead or buried alive in the wreckage*, I'm on my stomach and the arm wrapped around my face tastes like a gritty lemon paste, smells like orange bubble gum, like Circus Peanuts. Light breaks open in my brain and shines on the back of my eyes, exposing broken vessels, tired retinas. Shock therapy in my arteries, buzzing like a blank radio and numb like a sleeping foot. I'm stuck here, roped and blocked with his fingers up my ass. No, wait, did I tell the fucking part already? How did I start this story?

Late at night, I drive out to the docks and stare out into the lake. And it feels like I'm drifting out, away from the shore, away from everything. I lie on my back, settle down in one of the concave places, rub my fingers against the wood. And the night gets so dark that I can't see anything. Even my hands, inches from my face.

And then I start falling asleep, but it feels different than this in-and-out stuff. I feel my body letting go. Uncontrolled, unconscious, uncomfortable. And no matter how hard I try, no matter how much I tug and grunt at the stupid ropes, I know that I'm about to go under.

And this beautiful creature with the tiny mustache, orange-scented forearms and perfectly drawn lips breaks open another bottle of clear something and stuffs the needle down into it. "Want another one?" he says.

I roll my head back, willing it all away, trying to scream into the void, but nothing comes out. All the hairs on my neck bolt upright, there's a continuous crackling of dendrites in my brain. I try to jerk away, and then—

Quiet.

I come out of it, shaken and unsure. The borders of the room materialize again, walls and windows and doors. And this grease monkey climbing up on top of me. And the hand is gone, the air sealed again, impermeable, like a see-through plastic surface.

And once more, the blazing white light of the needle going down into my skin.

My arms go limp, the rope slacks.

My eyelids atrophy, fail.

# FUCKING DOSEONE

## Ralowe Trinitrotoluene Ampu

*For Dax Pierson, my sexy one-time assigned processing correspondent*

Doseone said something really weird and homophobic at an Anticon show when he was freestyling. It was at 26 Mix. It made me really angry. I keep talking about it. I get so emotional. As a rapper, I feel like I need to create my own history: points in a time line of some personal significance, the way De La Soul tried to manufacture a consumer history on *Stakes Is High* by opening the album with the question, Where were you when you first heard "Criminal Minded"? I went to this fateful Anticon show around when I first started rapping seriously, and Dose was one of the first real rappers I'd ever met. I ran into him at Amoeba Records on Telegraph Avenue in Berkeley. I suppose he still works there. I was browsing when I saw him out of the corner of my eye. White boy. White T-shirt. Glasses.

I grew up in Ventura, in an all-white suburb of Southern

California, a sprawling, desolate expanse of tract homes. I lived there for twenty-one years and it made me really angry. Telegraph Avenue near the UC Berkeley campus reminds me of Ventura. And Dose reminds me of the white boys across the street who used to call me *nigger*. They were the first kids I made friends with.

I'm wandering around Telegraph when I start writing about desire, or maybe childhood. I see a group of young, pouty white boys fully nigga'ed-out in saggy sweat suits and I imagine their dicks in my mouth as they cast shady glances at me, just barely giving me enough sidewalk. There are also mall boys, with asymmetrical rocker hair, wearing Leon Neon bracelets and sports coats, angel blue eyes wracked with pain. Looks like they've just gotten dropped off by their parents. There's a feeling of a constant sea of frustrated desire. My pornographic imagination is utterly overloaded by the ebb and flow to and from the Berkeley campus.

Dose was superfriendly. My hand was hovering above MF Doom, and Dose came over and was all, like, "That's a good album," then produced another from a row of CDs. "This is, too." Then, "Actually, this is *my* album. Hi, I'm Adam." When I realized I had seen Doseone perform before at Rico's in downtown San Francisco, I said, "Your stuff sounds like Solesides," and Dose said, "Lyrics Born was one of the first rappers that opened up to me." I told her I was in Deep Dickollective, a black gay rap group, and I gave her my group's URL, and she gave me her email at Dirtyloop. I ended up at Amoeba the next day because my friend Lyndon wanted to shop for CDs and I ran into Dose again. I was, like, "Hmm, you work a lot." She asked me again what I meant about being in a gay rap group. The concept seemed to evade her. Doscone had listened to a D/DC EP, and was perplexed by our apparent homophobia, demanding to know,

"Are you gay?" and I said for the third time, "Yes." I didn't realize that Dose might be indicating an insight into the fallacy of D/DC's hypermasculine performance; I was also caught up in it.

Doseone's show began with a freestyle battle where Sage Francis and Pedestrian abandoned their "conscious and experimental" rap style to imitate the homophobic remarks of ignorant rappers. At that time I was too stunned by the literal homophobia in it to register that it was also obviously racist. Then Doseone did "Spin Classes" and "innovation in the field of breath" and her verse from the second side of *cLOUDDEAD apt. A*, and I thought it was the most amazing thing I'd heard in my life. He was combining the dark, bleak insanity of early Tricky, the insular self-sustained inventiveness of De La Soul's first albums, and raw Freestyle Fellowship improvisational shit straight out of the old Good Life Café open mike in South Central Los Angeles. He took these and infused them with his own particular experiences, creating something I'd never heard before. His delivery was completely inconsistent and unpredictable. He sounded so vulnerable and effeminate, performing the exact queer rap style I'd been cultivating. But then Dose freestyled in this weird mannish voice: "I've been to college / did my four years / it's like a penitentiary / except no queers...." I mean, he actually said that.

There are queers at colleges. I've had sex with them in the bathroom at Cal, right up the street from where Adam "Doseone" Drucker works.

Up Telegraph from Amoeba Records, go through Sather Gate across the bridge, and on your left stands Dwinelle Hall. Downstairs in the men's bathroom there's a stall from which one can see anyone entering the bathroom. There's a flood of human masturbation material making its way to the basement between classes. It's funny to speculate which people have the weakest alibi for coming into this particular remote bathroom. There are two or three bathrooms on every floor of Dwinelle. Can this many obvious faggots all have to pee here at the same time? And these girls are not closet cases, but, like, straight-up *Queer As Folk* wannabes. They give something away in their overdetermined attempt to identify as casual when peeing. Once, I saw a very proper queen wearing a tear-away snap-up sweats athletic ensemble, pretending to be jockish. I cruised her with no subtlety at all. But I didn't allow her any space for pretense, so she lost sexual interest. She had her long, permed hair in a bob. And she had a fat cock with a thick head. I didn't get a chance to taste it.

Another time, I saw spiky, dark-haired twins with really beautiful eyes and pretty, reddish pink lips. Nothing makes me cum harder than boys' lips. I have an early memory of being repulsed by a kiss on the cheek from some random matron at my church. That repulsion swelled when my next-door neighbor (and best friend), a white boy named Steven, tried to kiss me on his front lawn. I pushed him away. His family moved to Taiwan shortly afterward and I never saw him again. I've spent the rest of my life overcompensating. Maybe I'll find him, and his lips, here. My ex-boyfriend Jo-ey had really full lips that would engorge when he was aroused; when I masturbate, thinking about the sex we used to have, I recall the soft fleshy cushion of his lips as we kissed and jerked each other off. So I fantasize kissing and jerking off with these twins, whose lips are delicate and shaped like a dove's wings. Actually, I don't think they were cruising, but that doesn't stop me from imagining that their erect cocks are the same color as their lips, and I want to watch them 69-ing each other.

Time passes. Enough time for the smallest details to become

exaggerated to manic-depressive extremes. Feelings of rejection seem like a well-grounded justification for suicide. Why am I participating in this hunting range of masculinity? But then a stern, frumpy white boy stands at the urinal with his eyes fixed on mine, through the crack in my stall door. I stand up to get a better look, with my cock in my hand as the blood that was trapped in my thighs by the toilet seat circulates from toes to head once more. I open the door with my pants unzipped so that my hard cock juts out, and I walk over to a urinal a couple down from this boy's. His face is pale and his lips are pink-rose colored and fixed at an attitude that's a mixture of pride and bewilderment. His thick glasses stand on the end of a pointy nose. His cock is of a compulsive-masturbating-nerd thickness, with a beautiful veiny shaft, and his cockhead is throbbing. I'm in love. I move to stand next to him and we start jerking each other off.

Someone comes in and we snap back into place apart from each other and pretend to finish peeing. The intruder is in his mid-forties, dressed like she's getting ready for a hiking trip through leather country with the Sierra Club; she's a regular whom I recognize immediately. The frumpy white boy zips his hard-on away, a huge and conspicuous bulge in the crotch of his pants, and leaves the bathroom in embarrassment. The way he knew precisely where to look into my stall convinces me that he's only pretending to be embarrassed. I follow her out of the bathroom and can't figure out which way she went, so I guess. I leave Dwinelle and I spot the boy by the library. I trail him past the clock tower and toward buildings I don't recognize, while maintaining what I feel to be a discreet distance. I assure myself that I'm not stalking her. She's going to show me another cruise spot and then we'll have the most amazing sex of our lives. But I lose her in some kind of science faculty building. On this occasion I don't feel suicidal because I'm not really depressed, since she hasn't actually rejected me. Just to be sure, I check every bathroom in this new building. I convince myself that this guy's locked away in his professor's office, leaking semen from his pulsing fire extinguisher cock while surfing porn online at an old wooden desk, and shooting all over his own face and lips. I wonder if he takes his glasses off first.

Back at Dwinelle, the air is calm, at a nearly *in utero* temperature. The fluorescent lights buzz dream-like, and there's all that tile. When you get a stranger's grooming habits, moisture, and intent stuck under your skin, it's really hard to shake loose. I'm sitting in a stall trying to either meditate or go into hibernation when the stall door next to me opens and closes. I peer through the hole where a bolt once held the toilet paper dispenser in place, and see a hot, skinny gay boy, wearing sports vintage, furiously stroking his cock. His arms are lean and toned and I think I see a couple of circuit tats peeking gingerly from under the sleeve of his off-yellow T-shirt. I get on the floor and stick my hard pre-cum-slicked cock underneath the stall partition and he starts sucking me off—just above par. I fuck his mouth but someone enters the bathroom and we both hop onto our respective thrones until it's clear, and then start again, until he stands and strokes his fat cock while watching someone else enter. After they leave he continues to stand, and I can see from his shadow that he's stroking his cock wistfully. This strikes me as forlorn.

I look under the partition at him to let him know that I want to suck him off. His petite features suggest to me that he's mixed race, perhaps with a little black somewhere, who knows, also thick eyebrows and a very blank gay lifestyle expression on his young face. He crouches and begins to lay his cock on my lips when someone else enters the bathroom. This happens several times. I spot drool below the partition of the stall wall.

It registers that it's mine. Or maybe his? I look through the bolt hole and see him dabbing spit on his cock, or maybe tasting his own pre-cum; I can't tell which. She stands up again, stroking her cock, watching someone who's now at the far urinal. I sit back on my toilet seat and try to see who it is. It's another gay boy, Latino I think, with extremely present thick-lashed brown eyes that are intensely affecting innocence. She has full, florid lips parted in a lascivious attitude, lips that she alternately licks and bites in a roller-coaster–riding fashion. He has a crew cut and strikes me as beefy but in a jock sort of way and she's also wearing a bright red long-sleeved T-shirt that says, "I'm a Pepper!" between erect nipples across her broad chest. She stands back and starts stroking a surface-to-air missile-shaped dick with a bright red tip shooting from the fly of her unbuckled jeans after we—that is, the gay boy in the stall next to me, and I myself—simultaneously open our doors so that he can see us stroking our cocks. I notice that his cockhead is pinker than his lips, more the color of his tongue. And then *someone else* enters the bathroom. Busy afternoon. I slam my door as the new person walks to the sink.

I peek through the crack. It's another gay boy, brown hair and blue eyes, with maybe freckles and an abrupt set of lips. He has a patient look. He's wearing a blue lacrosse jersey. I'm not sure how I know at first that it's a lacrosse jersey, but then I realize everybody is wearing Abercrombie. The gay boy with the red Abercrombie shirt is cruising the gay boy with the blue Abercrombie shirt, who starts rubbing a bulge in the baggy crotch of his Abercrombie cargo shorts. I open my stall door and find that my neighbor, with her yellow Abercrombie tee, has opened hers too.

My revulsion at being so breathlessly aroused by not just gay boys, but by gay boys wearing Abercrombie, starts fucking with my head. I find myself stroking and squeezing my cock just to continue appearing aroused. I start having a panic attack and faintly notice the sound of pants being ankle-dragged across the floor. I look down at the blue Abercrombie shirt gay boy's shoes. I divert myself with objective class analysis, to cool my panic attack. The other gay boys' shoes are new and sporty, but blue is going in the other direction—his couture is not as new or together as the other boys' mall ensembles. I observe that she has the sensible yet unfortunately unkempt dark brown hair of someone who doesn't like thinking about it. She's dressed like someone would want to dress if they aspired to dress just like someone who's part of the universal Caucasian-gay-person standard for the ruling class working at being working class—and therefore bound to a conservative utilitarianism that only hints at originality, because perhaps his resources aren't adequate to acquire the correct brand of boring shoe, so she could only get that which was within reach, so that his shoes are only almost (but not yet completely) boring.

At last I admit to myself that nobody is paying attention to me, or my runaway class analysis. I leave the bathroom.

After I rapped with D/DC at Wesleyan, I went from Connecticut to Pittsburgh with DDT. I played Greenthink and cLOUDDEAD for her. She was a fag, and thought it sucked. Now she likes it and tells me she appreciates their playful and inventive dissonance. At that time, working with her did not go as planned. After she told me I had no rhythm, I wandered around an area of Pittsburgh called Oakland and went to a cruisy business school auditorium basement bathroom and saw a tag that read *Dose-1* in blue marker. It was like Dwinelle, but even busier. I noticed that here too there were more gay boys than people who looked like they were in the closet. When you entered the bathroom there was an anteroom and another door. This door led around a bend to a row of urinals. Next to that was a row of toilet stalls in a corner of the bathroom that seemed intentionally to not be as well lit as the rest. I came through briefly and fell in love, like, six times, but had to hurry to go see a nice distracting Hollywood movie with DDT since I had abandoned any hope of collaborating with him.

However, I remembered the tag. True, it could've belonged to anyone. But I know that Dose went to business school. I wrote lyrics to it in the song I made with DDT right before he decided that I had no rhythm.

Bathrooms, bathrooms. So imagine my shock when Dose starts talking from behind me in the john.

"Is this an oblivion check?" I coo.

Okay, hold on a second....

I can tell you're wondering if I'm going to fuck Doseone. Well, I'm not sure. I remember the time before this that I ran into him. Eric was there. Eric is white and in Gay Shame with me. Eric and I were standing in front of Modern Times Bookstore in San Francisco after our Saturday Gay Shame meeting, and we were processing how she was upset about the Queer Anarchist People of Color group's having a meeting at the same time as ours, and spreading too thin the identical group of people who do radical queer direct action, and not wanting to be in a group without people of color. Doseone walked up with his friend. He was wearing camouflage cargo shorts. I hate camouflage and I hate cargo shorts. He said hi, and I was *so* not in any kind of space to deal with Dose at that second because I was really concerned with the issues that Eric was raising. What was so striking about this moment was that symbols for everything in the world that I felt strongly about were intersecting and converging with astronomical intensity. So I was taken aback. Dose asked what was going on and I said that Eric and I had just come out of a Gay Shame meeting. Eric later scolded me for saying to Dose that Gay Shame is a radical queer direct action group that focuses on "homophobia and assimilation in the gay community," when actually our focus is a lot broader than that, but I was panicking. As I fucked up my explanation of what Gay Shame was about, Dose interjected his opinions: when I said "homophobia," he said "and nonhomophobia?" in an oddly contentious manner. This was as close to a freestyle battle as I'd ever want to get into with Doseone. So while talking, I was also thinking: *Oh shit, Dose is going to serve me on this curb.* But I didn't have the presence of mind to turn to Doseone and say: "Dose, I was really annoyed about that song where you talk about the city—you appear to have no interest in the real systematic and historic dynamics that create divisions among people and cause tension in urban settings. I find it really problematic to suggest that all that oppressed and disenfranchised people in the city need to do is say, 'Let it be said dead butterfly' and 'Where's the love?' and then all these larger issues will be solved. But you mention nothing about these larger issues. Like, never in your music. Anywhere. Why?"

I did have the presence of mind to notice that Dose had not introduced his friend, a woman. She watched our interaction with a staid but not unpleasant expression. I snatched the opportunity to introduce myself to her, in an attempt to expose what, in all fairness, could have been either social awkwardness or male chauvinism...or maybe male chauvinism masquerading as social awkwardness. Then Dose disappeared into the store with his female companion.

* * *

But back to the bathroom.

"Is this an oblivion check?" I coo.

Dose asks, "So, you're still making music with Gay Shame?"

"Gay Shame doesn't make music. That would be Deep Dick-ollective. And no. I do solo stuff. D/DC has no politics."

I hate being black…. Dose senses my energy. I interpret some-thing in the rhythm of his pauses and the direction of his atten-tion as some type of contentious male competitive athlete drama. It's a rapper thing. It's a performance cue. Our interaction, my instincts tell me, is probably not going to be conducive to any preperformance preparation rituals Dose may have…. Searching his eyes, I find myself wondering about how I read paragraphs in *The Brothers Karamazov* and imagine that Dose has read the same shit. And I want to talk to him about the book for hours. Shrug and lie around devouring poetic discovery, holding each other, kissing in Ventura, or something….

"Yeah…they're really liberal."

"I guess you think I'm liberal, too," Dose says.

"Yes, I do."

My hands drop and I sputter.

"There's no soap."

"I think you're supposed to just scald them, then."

"Ah, c'mon. Don't. That seems judgmental."

"Of course it is. Judgment is a function of intelligence."

"Why're you so mad all the time?" Doseone says, and then I'm, like, well…. I do the thing I do when I turn tricks. I'm unex-pectedly calm. It's a new feature of my reasoning. I'm looking at the surface of Dose's mouth, and I'm imagining something outside the arty white-trash-chic unseemliness of the press photos, or accidental passings on the sidewalk. His lips look like desiccated bus bumpers, I imagine from years of unchecked alcohol and ecstasy consumption. Suddenly his flesh is demystified and it's just flesh. And then I start thinking about how something standing still can turn into something else. I want to vitiate the spirited message board claims—oh, there was quite an uproar on the Anticon message board, now defunct, on the subject of my outcry against the 26 Mix incident: claims that all my noise was nothing more than reaction to my spurned, star-crazed love for Doseone.

I'm watching for what Dose decides to do, feeling not so much cornered as completely blank and ready. I mean, if there's anything you want. If I give it to you, that doesn't make you a thief. Does it become less interesting? The me-offering-it part? Examining the rest of his body, of nearly identical stature to mine, how it would look contorted in the act of coming, contorted like when he performs. "Yes, y'all. If you got the cock I got the balls." I'm eager to be present for whatever happens in this bathroom at the LoBot Gallery in West Oakland. The idea gets me off. I do want to fuck Doseone. Out of spite for the bathroom in the basement of the David Lawrence Auditorium at Pittsburgh University where I saw *Dose-1* tagged next to a glory hole. In the song I wrote with DDT, I confused Pittsburgh U with Carnegie Mellon U. Both are in Oakland, PA, not to be confused with Oakland, CA, where Anticon is now based. The *Dose-1* tag struck me because there were no other tags next to it.

I wandered around the Pittsburgh campus using an online tip. Being from California and really bad at geography in general, I didn't realize that Pennsylvania was sandwiched between Ohio and New Jersey. Doseone met up with Odd Nosdam and Why? in Cincinnati to collaborate on Greenthink and cLOUDDEAD. Doseone writes about growing up in New Jersey. I didn't really realize where I was. I've always kind of wondered if the tag was really Dose's. And what was he doing in that bathroom?

The bathroom in the basement of David Lawrence Auditorium was really busy when I first passed through, but when I came back it was dead. I was hurrying out the door from using the sink when a boy zipped past me, meeting my eyes. I paused before the stairs leading up into the main lobby of the auditorium. My eyes were drawn to a poster about something Islamic plastered on the fake wood paneling; my mind danced elsewhere, wondering about the boy. I returned to the bathroom, imagining that if I walked a certain way he wouldn't know by the sound of my footsteps that I was the same person. He was alone in the toilet stall with the glory hole and Dose's tag. I shuffled to the stall next to his. Through the glory hole, I could see his arm moving up and down and then stopping. I was crazy hard. I unzipped my fly and pulled out my cock. Its tip was shiny.

Instead of entering the other stall, I peeked through the crack of his door. His head was down. He seemed embarrassed. I stood back and displayed my rigid pulsing cock, swinging it until he looked up. His face was pudgy and cute. He appeared to be half Asian, half white. His lips were small and angular. His eyes were wide, looking first at my cock then into my eyes, then back. I pulled my shirt up and tweaked my nipples. He opened his legs and sat back on the toilet, stroking his cock anew. He stood and moved his backpack from the hook on the stall door and set it on the floor. He pulled his shirt over his head and opened the stall door. I stepped closer, squeezing my pre-cumming cock. Something about the earnest artlessness of his red mohawk suggested to me that he wasn't a gay boy just yet, but had been reading a couple of books on gay theory while listening to downloads of Tracy and the Plastics. His cock was medium sized, pointy, and uncut, with a shiny bright-pink hammerhead. I leaned over and sucked the salty, sticky dripping pre-cum collected under his foreskin. He panted, frantically bucking his hips into my face. His cock throttled in my cheeks and I grabbed his ass to force it deeper, to choke me. I exhaled and I stood up and we kissed, stroking our cocks together in saliva and pre-cum.

I liked how his body was pudgy and not gym-toned to death, in contrast to an actual gay boy's. I did frown at the spiked belt, which to me seemed to hint at the misfortune to come. We shot at the same time, spraying both the glory hole and Doseone's tag.

But back to the bathroom at LoBot Gallery in West Oak-land.

Doseone is wearing camouflage again, which I deplore above all things in the world; this time it's a camouflage trucker cap. How can Dose have any antifascist critique in his work while unthinkingly choosing to adorn his person in the costume of the military? Here I could win an argument about the ineffectiveness of a liberal ideology. I look at Dose and feel so utterly self-conscious about my art. I remember doing the new listening stations at Amoeba that played *Deep Puddle Dynamics* and feeling every strained syllable of my D/DC delivery and body language on stage, how I would channel Dose's inflections. Then I remember the past. Taking my ex-boyfriend to the Imusicast show. Sure, Jo-ey was cuter than Dose—because clearly Jo-ey's lips were at that time a great deal more hydrated and healthy than Dose's chain-smoker lips—but I think how an obsession with intention and technique had half-filled the time since I last had a boyfriend. Planning my alibi as the Black Doseone, the triple irony of a black person impersonating a white person impersonating a black person.

So we're letting the silence pass in the bathroom and I'm witnessing the impression of Dose's nipples rising up through his nonsweatshop Subtle T-shirt. It's so hip-hop to wear a T-shirt with your band's name on it that's the same as the one you sell.

"I wanna suck your cock," I finally say.

"You should come to the after party," Dose says without a beat.

"Now."

"No sex before the show."

"What kind of a rock star *are* you?"

"I'm not a rock star. I'm a poet."

"Rock star poet."

"No sex before the show," Doseone says again, and leaves the bathroom, just as someone enters.

I retreat to the handicapped stall. I think: *Freedom penis dipping in a toilet of tears.* It's the hot white boy I saw on his cell phone in the street coming to LoBot. Where do these people *come* from? This one has sideburns. I've been especially enamored of sideburns lately. You know, I had a dream about this white boy before. In it he's peeing and glances around to find me looking at him. He slips into the stall next to mine. I look under the stall wall at him and he starts jerking off. But I came before he got there, just from looking at him, so it's too late, and then I wake up.

But this hot cell phone white boy has come into the bathroom to gaze into the mirror. Using the mirror takes her a long time. On the back of her baggy T-shirt is a picture of Bub Rubb going "Whooooo-whoooooo!" White boys love their Internet objectification of black people, don't they? I find my cock tender and semihard as, for an improbable duration, this boy preens herself in the mirror, just for me. I masturbate, studying her from inside my stall while she anoints her insanely smooth and clear face. She has such good skin. "The no-place of an ache dangles body all around it," Dose wrote. The sordid and masochistic suburban identification...a body in a mirror. "See me," I think, as finally being seen feels as close as touching a streetlamp light bulb from a seat on the train poised on the aerial track over a neighborhood in West Oakland. He'll see me in five seconds. I'm lost because all I can think is, "She'd come into the stall next to me in a split second if I was white." Conqueror. The giving is dripping off every muscled hormonal gland and pore in my feverish, abject flesh. Or: "He'd kiss me if I was white." I'm giving every part of my sweaty, mathematical lucubration, tightening around a pencil to go over some really pornographic diagnostics of what it is to want to slide into some skin with a couple of years knocked off mine, to feel whatever unthinkable thing is happening between self and image; to be taking careful stock of all the bone-structured angles that have never experienced worry, never drifted, never been alienated out of the confines of their own extravagant symmetry. Whiteboy: check! Hegemony: check! It's there…yet remote, desirable. "It's the boy in me that binds a worldly, gutted man's angst to change. Celebratory delta paints shit-eating grins on what you and mirrors think my face looks like." New clothes, she puts her camouflage trucker hat on, slightly off center. They must be giving them away tonight. I hate being black. I do. My cock, trembling hard, continues to drip, and my sense of history numbs. All I can see is locked suburban rooms in rows by the thousands, TV sets, a breathing semidark, and hard white cocks and faces flushed the same color. "Johnny Cock Rocket!" I recite. Skateboard, a doll-like face with impossibly blushed blood-colored lips and ocean-colored eyes…and what I do with my dick disappears into a racial Ventura rewrite, history is traded for a second of an orgasmic pang of oppressive escapism, hardening my resolve to unmake the world like a slap in the face. For exactly one instant it occurs to me that I know the precise and obvious words that would unmake the world. The moment fades. It takes me, like, two seconds to come.

# THE STRAY

David May

*Some are more human than others.*
—Stevie Smith

Bud was discovered, as strays often are, wet, cold, and shivering in the back patio of the Seattle Eagle. It was commonly assumed that Bud had had parents and a family at some time in his life, and even a proper name, but none of this information was forthcoming. Stories spread rapidly that he'd been kidnapped and imprisoned and had only just managed to escape with his life, but with no memory of life prior to his enslavement (for cable television had supplied numerous such stories to draw on); or that he was the victim of some cruel Master who, having provided Bud with a brain injury, abandoned his amnesiac slave to Fate. While none of the scenarios being woven about his past proved to be true, neither was there ever a satisfactory explanation of Bud's beginnings.

The facts were these: the day manager found Bud huddled in

the back of the bar's patio. Being a kind man, the day manager knelt beside him and asked, "What's your name, bud?"

And from that moment, he answered to Bud.

The bar's manager and staff then took it upon themselves to look after Bud, to feed and clothe him, to keep him warm and safe—just until he was able to tell them what had happened. Bud, it should be noted, had an almost unearthly handsomeness, with a compact, well-muscled, furry body; high cheekbones, and devastating green eyes complemented by a sexy scruffiness that appeared permanent. Being that sexy and that handsome, as well as agreeable, his presence was something of a commodity. Soon Bud was working at the door of the Eagle on weekends and sometimes as a towel boy at the bathhouse across the street. Customers were charmed by his guileless pleasure in being admired, to say nothing of his willingness to provide whatever pleasure his admirers might ask of him. Thus he was treated kindly, as strays often are when they are both beautiful and agreeable.

In no time, he was collared and well cared for by a Sir who saw in Bud all that was wild and wonderful in the world. He treated Bud gently but firmly, and Bud thrived under his care. Already free with his body, Bud had no qualms about repaying the Sir's kindness with whatever sexual reciprocation was required of him. Sir loved Bud deeply, and when he learned that he had pancreatic cancer, he took steps to be certain that someone would take care of Bud after his death.

When Sir died, Bud didn't weep, but uttered primal cries of despair. He wandered about the apartment looking for someone he knew would never return, burying his face in Sir's pillow and finding comfort in what remained of the man's scent. He was adopted then, as strays frequently are when orphaned, by Sir's friends, a couple known as the Bills. Bud slept between them, or in a pile of blankets on the floor, accepting their attentions, sexual and otherwise, with a kind of acquiescence that they found touching. In addition to cleaning house for the Bills (and Bud was nothing if not obsessed with cleanliness) and working in their garden, Bud continued to work at the Eagle on weekend nights, as a bathhouse towel boy on other nights, and as a purveyor of pleasure when the occasion arrived. Downstairs in the Bills' playroom, Bud built himself a nook to sleep in. Closeted there, snug and secure in the dark he felt at home in, he slept through most of Seattle's wet winter days. When the weather was fine, he slept naked, stretched out across a blanket on the back lawn, abandoning himself to the sun as if it were his only lover.

Late at night Bud would wander Capitol Hill, deftly leaping into trees, padding gently across rooftops, or gracefully running along back fences. When the moon was full, he would sit on the rooftop and stare at it for hours, finding comfort in the cold light and the smells of the night. Then he'd stretch, and gracefully, almost silently, leap to a tree, then the fence, and finally the wet, dewy earth. Shaking the pads of his feet dry, Bud quietly returned to the warmth of the Bills' bed, where he would sleep succored by the scent and warmth of the men who had taken over his care.

When awake, Bud watched the world around him with constant curiosity, alert to subtle shifts in his surroundings. He listened carefully to every word said within his earshot, sometimes repeating what had been said word for word weeks, or even months, later. Other than these few odd habits (odd habits not being uncommon among strays), Bud smiled when expected to smile and laughed when it was proper to laugh. In short, he seemed not quite normal, but normal enough, and content with his life.

Years passed, and one May the Bills decided to take Bud with them to Chicago for International Mr. Leather. They had gone in previous years, off and on, but had been disinclined to spend their money on Bud's airfare and food, leaving Bud at home to take care of himself. When they returned, Bud was happy to see them, seeking some sign of affection—a slap on the ass, a cock down his throat, a fierce dry fuck while he bent over the toilet—to assure himself that he was still loved. This year, however, the Bills realized that they were losing their edge, having passed the peak of their appeal as Daddies, and decided to bring Bud with them, thus securing for themselves the status of Slave Owners, and so increasing their desirability.

Bud did not take easily to being on a leash, but complied despite his desire to run free. Being led about, dressed in new gear (rubber, leather, camouflage), on display, was not something he was well suited to, but neither was being punished, so he obeyed. Not liking the crowds at the event, Bud would, when surrounded by so many admiring strangers, lean into one or both of the Bills for safety. For this he was teased but fondly caressed, and so it became a part of his strategy for survival in the noisy vastness of the hotel's lobby. That the Bills sometimes sold his ass to strangers was of less concern to him than that he not be restrained or caged, so he remained docile while keeping an eye on the exit, a ploy common to strays whose survival depends on the kindness of others.

Late Saturday night, after an orgy that might have exhausted others (an orgy to which the Bills' entrance had only been made possible by their ownership of so beautiful a boy), Bud's owners collapsed into bed, snoring away almost as soon as their heads hit their pillows. Bud, accidentally left unfettered for the night, removed the leash and most of his clothes before exploring the halls and stairwells of the enormous hotel. He sniffed the air hoping to find what he was looking for, what he sensed was waiting for him.

He found men in every out-of-the-way corner, singly or in groups, wherever he looked, men unused to so much stimulus and unable to sleep for fear they miss something, men stumbling back to their beds after a night of dreamlike debauchery, men waiting in the doors of their rooms hoping for one more fuck. Some of these men reached out to him, called to him with thick, urgent voices, but Bud ignored them. They were not what he sought; they were not the one he knew was so near.

He entered the lobby bar with reluctance, even as his instincts urged him forward. A good number of men still congregated there during the late hour, some of them sad enough to earn Bud's sympathy. He moved lithely through the milling men, eyes and ears alert. Some were laughing too loudly, some sobbing into oversized cocktails over a lover's faithlessness; others basked in the glow of so many men, absorbing the pheromones that filled the air. And there, in the center of it all, was the one Bud sought, the one he'd sensed was there since his arrival two days before.

Bud stood and stared. The man stared back.

The man was tall, powerfully built, thick legged, and almost impossibly muscular. His sandy blond mane of thick hair was in need of cutting; a full beard covered his face almost up to the cheekbones. His mouth was large and sensual; his brown eyes glinted yellow when the light caught them; his bare arms, chest, and back were thickly matted with fur.

Someone said something funny, and he laughed, his laugh a roar, his chuckle a very loud purr. Surrounded by admirers, the man accepted their homage with a graceful acquiescence, gently touching one or another of them in their conversation, slapping another manfully on the back. Through all this cama-raderie, though, he remained aloof, waiting as he was for Bud to find him. Very calmly leaving his flock of admirers, the stranger approached Bud, gently touching the small of Bud's back, stepping close to Bud before whispering, "There's my little bro."

Bud's heart stopped in his throat.

"Are you my brother?"

"You didn't know?"

"Big bro?"

"That's right."

There was a kiss, gentle and deep, strong and tender, that laid claim to Bud as neither Sir nor the Bills had ever done. Big Bro put a hand on Bud's tightly covered ass and walked away with him amidst the applause, the *ohs* and *ahs* and laughter of those who had hoped for Big Bro's attention and now wished that they could watch the coupling to come.

Big Bro led Bud out of the hotel and hailed a cab. Nearly naked, Bud wrapped himself around Big Bro more for protection than for warmth in the night's quite cool spring air, hiding what was exposed from an uncertain world. The cab raced along the lake, Bud nestling into the vast furriness of Big Bro's chest, Big Bro stroking Bud's scruffy cheeks and chuckling so loudly that it sounded more than ever like a purr.

When they reached their destination, a tower overlooking the lake, its height threatening to scrape the sky with fairy tale–like accuracy, Big Bro led Bud by the hand inside and up the elevator to a vista frequented more by birds than men.

Bud stared into the open space beyond the window for several minutes, watching the moon's reflection on the lake that was so much like a small sea. Big Bro wrapped his arms around Bud, nibbling Bud's ear, caressing Bud's nipples, purring.

"Is this my new home, Big Brother?"

"Yes, little bro. This is where you belong."

Bud knelt and removed his boots and socks, then the tight leather shorts that had been his only other clothing. Kneeling before Big Bro, he undid the button fly and pulled aside the leather jeans to better see what was to possess him. Unleashed suddenly from the confines of the leather, the thick phallus slapped Bud sharply across the face. Bud flinched slightly before opening his mouth and inhaling Big Bro's mammoth member to the root. Big Bro rocked back and forth on his booted feet, his gloved hands caressing the back of Bud's head as he pushed his cock in and out of Bud's throat.

"Oh, little bro, oh, little bro…"

The rhythm of the rocking increased in speed, and Big Bro's murmurs became more guttural. Holding the back of Bud's head, he fucked Bud's mouth long and hard until, screaming, he exploded and shot his seed down Bud's anxious and hungry throat. Bud felt the head of the cock expand and burst, felt the ribbons of manhood cascade down his throat, and he eagerly swallowed even as the still hard cock was removed from his mouth.

After Big Bro had come to himself and had caught his breath, he knelt down next to Bud and kissed him with more longing than he had before, with more desire, more love. He held Bud close, letting their furry pelts rub against each other, kissing Bud, licking the sweat from Bud's face and neck. Bud responded in kind, purring with pleasure at the rough texture of his lover's tongue as it scraped against his skin and fur. He helped Big Bro out of his boots, leather jeans, harness, armbands and gloves. Licking the hairy flesh as it was newly exposed, making Big Bro purr in return, Bud sought only to please him, to mark him as his own, even as Big Bro had marked him.

Big Bro dove into Bud's hairy ass, parting the furry cheeks with his huge paws while his tongue sought the musk of Bud's sex, the new center of his own joy. On his stomach, Bud felt the rough tongue pluming the depths of his fuck hole, and kneaded the carpet just as Big Bro's paws were kneading his buttcheeks. Bud lost himself in the pleasure of the grooming, of the bearded face against his furry buttcheeks, in the need mounting in his own loins.

Bud was roughly turned over onto his back, his legs wrapping themselves over Big Bro's broad, hirsute shoulders. Big Bro's cock found its target and entered the snug cavern where so many men had spilled their spawn, but which would now make room only for Big Bro's essence. He entered slowly, ever alert for whatever sensations were revealed in his lover's face, as eager to please as to be pleased. Bud gasped, only partly from the pain of being split so roughly apart, and partly from anticipation of the coming ecstasy. He nodded, and Big Bro pushed forward, slowly sliding into the hairy hole, into the depths of Bud's body and soul.

The scent of their pheromones thickened the air around them, adding to the urgency of their need to couple, to climax face-to-face, to know and share the agony of the coming climax. They kissed roughly as they fucked, their teeth clashing together while their tongues wrestled for control. Big Bro pushed forward as Bud met each thrust with his own, his cock arching high into the air as Big Bro's manhood drove deeper and faster into Bud's body.

They came together. Big Bro's cock once again exploded, expanding and stretching the confines of Bud's guts. With Big Bro's final thrust, Bud's body arched toward the ceiling as he ejaculated, covering them both with cum. What Big Bro couldn't catch in his mouth, he licked from the matted hair on Bud's body, even as Bud returned the favor by cleaning Big Bro's sweaty body.

They slept that night curled together on the floor, their bodies intertwined for the comfort of each other's company as much as for warmth in the now chilly room. When they awoke, Bud prepared their breakfast, after which they spent an hour grooming each other before a short nap. When Big Bro stretched his body, he found Bud at the window keenly watching high-flying birds race past the apartment. He nuzzled Bud from behind, his cock poking at its new home.

"How old are you, Big Bro?"

"Don't know. Why? Do you know how old you are?"

"No. I never bothered to count."

"Not to worry, little bro, Big Bro will look after you now. Big Bro will protect you and keep you safe, and Big Bro will never put you on a leash."

Bud leaned his torso forward and pushed his butt back to find and engulf Big Bro's cock. That was all he needed to know.

When the Bills woke up the next morning and found Bud had vanished, they wondered where he had gone, but didn't worry at first. As the hours passed, they became frantic, showing his picture to everyone and anyone. Finally, on the morning of their departure, someone recognized Bud from the fuzzy image on the mobile phone.

"Yeah, a couple nights ago he went off with this guy, big ol' lion of a guy."

"Where did they go?"

The man shrugged his shoulders and nodded to the front door of the hotel.

On the flight home, the Bills comforted themselves with the thought that strays sometimes disappear.

# MASS ASS

Robert Patrick

A boy at the baths
Opened legs thin as laths
     To invite any dick up his ass.
We clustered to fuck
This divine piece of luck,
     Ev'ry putz in the place hard as glass.

We had come off the streets
Hunting fuckable seats
     Scorning bars and the park's grubby groves,
Seeking nooky, not names
Or good spirits or games
     Where hot crotches abounded in droves.

The baths was alive
As if drones in a hive
     Had come crawling for all they could get.

We crowded the halls
With a buzz in our balls,
    But no honey was coming as yet.

We dropped down to see
That the steam room was free.
    There was no ass to catch unawares,
And none in the cool,
Under-used swimming pool.
    We returned to the hall-hell upstairs.

There were pungent perfumes
From occasional rooms
    But most doors were annoyingly shut
As their renters, like me,
Walked around cockily,
    Rather randomly roaming in rut.

Every man there possessed
What the others liked best,
    Whether asshole or hard-on or mouth,
But it looked like the nest
Never would come to rest,
    And all hopes of connections went south.

Though the usual thing
At the baths was to fling
    Your door open and get yourself some,
On a night like tonight
Everyone was uptight
    And nobody was likely to cum.

Every mind in the dim,
Dreamy den was a-brim
     With idyllic, ideal, unreal acts,
Which seemed to eclipse
Any real lips or hips
     Ever coming to grips with bare facts.

So the corridors sludged
As we judged as we trudged
     All around in the shadows in hordes,
And the testicles hung
In between our legs swung
     Full of seed as a garden of gourds.

When the cute youth came in
Through the masses of men,
     He was hot, clearly not there to swim,
For he stripped like a whore
In his wide-open door,
     And we all caught the heat off of him.

To conceal our rude dowels,
We were wrapped in white towels
     But the kid spread his out on his cot,
Then reclined on his back,
Plucked open his crack
     And inserted K-Y up his twat.

Just a blond, bonny boy,
Not in any way coy,
     Undulating gyrating crevasse,
Legs divided and bent

For to better present
    Frontally, cuntily, ass.

The towel was to catch
Any leaks from his snatch,
    All ejaculatory excess.
The thought of those drops
Seeping out of his chops
    Escalated the hall's horniness.

Then the kid closed his eyes,
Elevated his thighs,
    And commanded all cocks in to cum.
Elders bruited around,
"There's a butt wanting browned.
    Better get into line and get some."

Everybody had tongues.
Everybody had bungs.
    Everybody bore seminal pods.
But the catamite's blunt
Self-reduction to cunt
    Ratified ev'rybody as rods.

So I felt myself swell
And I said, "What the hell,"
    And got into the queue to give juice.
I stood with my hand
Underneath my towel, and
    Pulled my pud to be ready for use.

Soon a long line had formed
And we heard the kid stormed
   By the first fuck to enter his door.
How he moaned as the first
Of our company burst
   In his lubricious tube like a boar.

Now the atmosphere was
Brash and bawdy, a-buzz
   With the promise of pending release.
We were boys in a frat
Lucking out, looking at
   A communal, anonymous piece.

We were sailors in port,
Self-advancers at court,
   Soldiers eyeing a drunk in a bunk,
Groaning drones servicing
A great, glistening queen
   Amid sexual, insectual funk.

The kid was reduced
To a gap to get goosed
   By our prods with explosive intent.
As our chargers got charged
His behind was enlarged
   In our minds to a meat monument.

Race, religion, and class
Were dispelled by that ass
   With its massive and passive reproof
That, divested of duds,

We were all silly studs,
    Dumb containers for cum on the hoof.

Men who hardly would greet
If they passed on the street
    In divisive, diverse uniforms
Here were stripped of disguise,
Bound as bulls by the rise
    Of identical sensual storms.

In the backs of our brains
We discovered remains
    Of religions remote as we played
In a crude, incondite
Eleusinian rite
    That was once dignified and arrayed.

We were in Babylon,
Devotees duly drawn
    Toward rolling, controlling white buns
Of a sexual slave
Cleft to show his dark cave
    Where initiates got off their guns.

Deep in wells dug in rocks,
Persians cut off their cocks
    And their balls to become temple whores.
So the boy in the room
Had become a huge womb
    To seduce and reduce our gorged gores.

When such rites were proscribed,
Men were bullied and bribed
    To enact them, defying the state.
In a dark alley-way,
An asshole in Pompeii
    Scrawled the ritual *Show hard, make date.*

This religion, repressed,
Recrudesced and tumesced
    Any time that men gathered with men,
And in barracks and ships
The hot hole in the hips
    Was enjoyed as it always had been.

In Athenian heights
On particular nights
    Men would drink not to think as they sprawled,
Then dishevel their robes
To reveal hairy globes
    With a butthole that begged to be balled.

In Catullus's Rome
With the Capitol's dome
    Hanging, clanging that butt was a vice,
Men ate asses in baths,
Flouting all aftermaths
    Just to service each other's sweet splice.

After pagan defeats,
In monastic retreats
    Any pretty young novice was told
That he must grow a beard,

For the Fatherhood feared
>> That a fair face would get his ass poled.

In my southwestern land
Where the butthole was banned
>> As a joke not to be spoken of,
Cowboys wooed with the song,
"Nights are long, oh, so long.
>> Gotta get me somebody to love."

All of us in that line
To defile the divine
>> Waiting wound that we heard being had
Had been taught we'd be burned
In hot Hell if we yearned
>> To deliver a load in a lad.

But the fever of youth
Told the tenderer truth
>> That the cock had to cum in the crack,
So despite gods and laws
We were lined up because
>> Gut was good and we wouldn't turn back.

As engorgement peeled husks
Off the tips of our tusks,
>> Our sarongs bulged with prongs like pale fruits.
We all jerked uncontrolled
Through the waistband or fold
>> Of the towels that enshrouded our shoots.

We wankers in line,
Feeling phallic and fine,
    Gaily joked as we stroked our taut tools.
Buggers worshiping butt,
Shuffling stallions in rut,
    We all broke one of Everard's rules

As we tugged off our towels
Among manly avowals
    That the damned things were feeling too tight.
Uncontained cocks and balls
Sent their scents down the halls
    As we waited for nooky that night.

All the bored employees.
Police-force retirees,
    Saw us standing illicitly stripped
And were moved to object,
But retired from respect
    Of the god by whom all goads were gripped.

A drunk coming in,
Gaped to see naked men
    As he clawed with a key at his door,
And a dick brushed my butt
And my prick pushed a rut
    As we jostled toward our hot whore.

For, oh, what a mass
Of assailable ass
    Hung available there where we stood.
And oh, what a stock

Of respectable cock,
    And we wondered if maybe we should…

So we played as we pleased
With the asses we squeezed
    And the cocks that we teased in the gloom,
But we all knew we must
Hold our trophies in trust
    For the priestess oiled up in her room.

The drunk stumbled out,
Waving hard-on about,
    Looking funky and phallic and fine,
Then staggered to stand
Towel and tool in each hand
    At the end of the lumbering line.

Like great droplets of dew
Or thick globules of goo,
    Devotees shuffled forward like slaves
As the pricks who had spilled
Came out limp and fulfilled
    Like the undead released from their graves.

When a man entered in
To that vaginal den,
    Every aching erection would pulse,
Throbbing just on the verge
Of a seminal purge
    As we heard each hot cocksman convulse.

Every brain in the chain
Fucked again and again
    That vicarious, visualized slit.
Every act grew more quick
As each man felt his prick
    Growing closer and closer to it.

How I swallowed a laugh,
Stimulating my staff
    While forbidding my seed to disperse
In the glory and grief
Of suspended relief
    Not unlike certain techniques of verse.

Then a fucker came out
Drooling cum from his spout,
    And the cock before mine climbed the kid.
I ogled the mass
Of his big apple-ass
    Slapping happily as he slip-slid.

My genitals got
So unbearably hot
    That I let my hand slide to the tip,
For had I clutched the rod
I'd have shot out my wad
    Watching that big behind grind and grip.

I felt what he felt
As he made his dick melt
    In the ass that already was soaked,
And I wanted my stump

In his high-riding rump
   Which made mean little mouths as he poked.

I was wildly aroused
By the thought of what housed
   His exploring and goring extreme,
And I'd seen the huge knob
On his fat little lob,
   Just the thing to give gut a good ream,

And his heaving, hot hole
Writhing out of control
   Made my schlong long to ruin his rear,
And panting to pole
Someone in the male role
   Had me feeling incredibly queer.

I twiddled my glans
And the next willing man's,
   While I watched all I saw of the fun:
Just my forefucker's seat
And a pair of pale feet
   On his shoulders as he got his gun.

My pulse muttered, "I
Could cram into that guy
   To fuck him as he bucks in that bung,
And the next guy, you see,
Could get on and in me—"
   But I just squeezed my meat where it hung.

Never, ever before,
As I eyed his back door,
    Had I so longed to stuff a butt's yawn.
I was me, I was him,
We were us, we were them
    Who'd observe us in rut and climb on.

Universally male,
Universally hale,
    Universally under cock's curse,
Universally rapt,
Universally trapped,
    Yawning yoni was our universe.

So I watched my prior priest
In the butt of the beast,
    The upreared reliquary he raunched,
His desirable duff
Undulating to stuff
    Where so many lewd loads had been launched.

I was flexing my thighs.
There were tears in my eyes
    And my lips were parched dry from hot breath.
My pelvis was just
An amalgam of lust
    As he labored for his little death.

Then, when he'd gotten off,
He got off with a cough
    And came out with a whispered, "Hot shit."
Then my shadow obscured

The asshole that allured
    As I felt for, then fell into it.

Oh, the state of that hole
As I put in my pole!
    It was drippily, slippily wet,
More a sluice than a slice,
Or, to be more concise,
    As appealing as asshole can get.

For the thought of the cocks
That had shot molten rocks
    Up that gully that so fully gaped,
And their bouncing behinds
As they blew out their minds,
    Made it their poles and assholes I raped.

My vagina on view
As I fucked the foul flue,
    My buns billowing open and shut,
I muscled him mean,
For I envied that queen
    All the men who had been up his butt.

I was wholly aware
Of my hole in the air
    As I fucked in his slushy, hot mush,
And my knowing the next
Dick desired what I flexed
    Made me pop in that slop with a gush.

Then I sighed and half-swooned
And withdrew from the wound,
    Shoving by the next guy in the chain,
Grunting, "Fucking great gash,"
As I stalked off to splash
    In the shower and piss down the drain.

As I strolled the cell-block,
Looking now for rock cock,
    There were plenty of men still lined up
With their towels on their necks,
Salivating for sex
    Mad to add to the cum in the cup.

It was just a dark cell,
Not the heavenly hell
    Where I'd just been the man of all men.
But the line, it would seem,
Was still dreaming that dream,
    And the drunk guy was just going in.

They were zombies in thrall
To a mystical call
    Which no longer now beat in my bone,
And their queen a mere pawn
As I passed them by, drawn
    By a mystical call of my own.

I located by smell
A pitch-black orgy-cell,
    Where on hard cement platforms and shelves
Men beyond or above

Holding out for true love
    Polymorphously proffered themselves.

There I felt lots of rungs
And I smelt lots of bungs,
    Then I fell down ass-up on the floor
To get fucked by a crew
Of butt-fuckers whose goo
    I'd been fucking in minutes before.

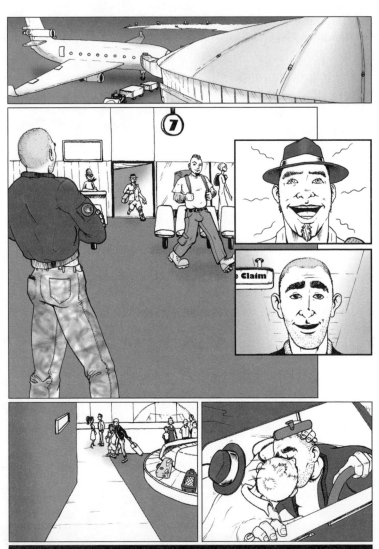

# The Welcome-Back Fuck

written by Dale Lazarov
drawn by Drub

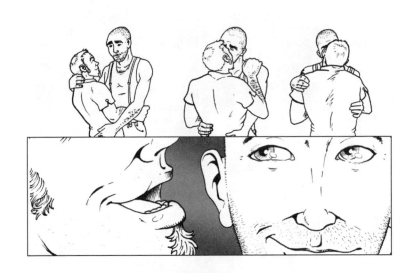

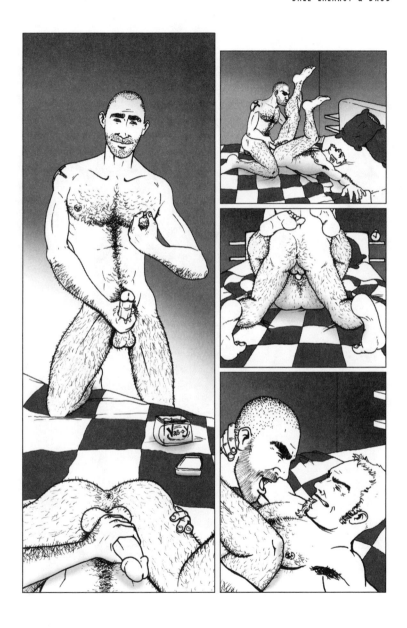

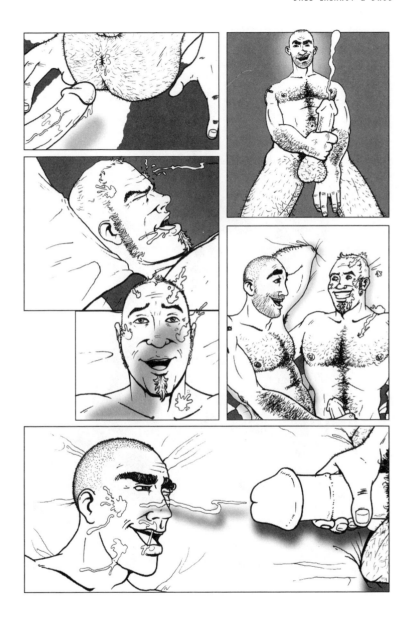

# TROUBLE LOVES ME

Steven Zeeland

Handsome young sailors half my age seduced me, gave me drugs, and pressured me to video-tape them performing lewd acts.

I never wanted to make a porn video. It happened by accident. With some help from the ghost of a beefcake photographer....

I know it sounds farfetched.

Running a background check on me will not likely make my claim appear any more immediately credible. My record includes authoring several books that could at first glance be mistaken for porn. Especially *Military Trade,* the cover of which depicts a nude Marine. And in various interviews I've called myself a "military chaser."

But only for want of a better term.

To the extent that I have it in me to be at all a predator, I have always ended up captured by the game.

*Bremerton, Washington—January 2001:*
  *Navy Stray Cat Blues*
  "Dude, I really need to jerk off."

I turn my head to meet the sailor's eye. But he suddenly looks worried at what he's just said and doesn't give me a chance to comment before hastily adding, "Hey, you don't mind me calling you 'dude'?"

Pro and I are lying on separate parallel couches, watching DVD porn on my living room TV.

I feign a frown. "No...."

Pro's accent is so subtle I don't really think of him as a Texan. But it occurs to me that back where he comes from young men still say "ma'am" and "sir." And that maybe he just now remembered that the year he was born I graduated high school.

"Why would I mind you calling me 'dude'?"

But before he can open his mouth I tell him that if he wants any lube, in the cabinet next to the TV he'll find three different varieties, and I add which brand I use.

Pro's preferences are not the same as mine. But he doesn't take offense at my using a petroleum-based lubricant.

Pro likes his lube slick and water-soluble. And the skin tone pixels he studies on my monitor are of a different body type.

My own gaze is less focused, intermittently shifts offscreen, and especially during the longer super-slow-mo intervals unabashedly favors his body.

Pro's body is flawless. His face is more handsome than any in my straight-porn DVD collection. He doesn't mind being admired with his shirt off and his jeans around his ankles.

But Pro isn't a hustler. And though the first time he visited me I paid him a respectable hourly rate for a test shoot in my studio, tonight he's not here as a model. We're just hanging out. My high-resolution digital camera is on the coffee table right next to me, and that's where it stays the whole time Pro masturbates. Until, that is, the very end.

"I'm just about there, dude."

"Pro, uh, do me a favor?"

A pause. Then, a low, flat, "What?"

I'm pretty sure I know what he's thinking. Something along the lines of *What the fuck? I should have known…. And just when I thought— Or maybe, God, I hope it's pictures of the money shot he wants.*

But one extraordinary quality I've already noted in Pro is his inimitable knack for shattering the ordinary. At random intervals, sufficiently infrequent to defy prediction yet somehow uncannily precisely timed, he'll do or say something so off the wall as to utterly floor you. But so casually, and so adroit and so fleeting, that in the second it takes you to register and look to his face for some sort of accounting, you find yourself confounded by "the neutral face of the Buddha" (which is far and away the only trait of the insatiably desiring Pro even remotely suggestive of the Buddha). And Pro, for his part, has already declared his admiration for my own offbeat "edge."

"I think we need to do something symbolic to mark this night. Would you mind ejaculating on my TV screen?"

Pro almost manages to not smile. "Are you sure?"

The monitor in question is a new, pricey, flat-screen Sony. A gift from a patron.

"Yes. I want to photograph your semen dripping down the screen."

Pro gives my TV a copious "facial." After he leaves the room to wash up I snap three shots and stare at the screen speculatively, wondering how much this AWOL sailor's spunk would taste of the strychnine-rich methamphetamine he shared with me twelve hours ago (my first experience with street drugs since the 1980s).

Pro steps back into the room.

"Dude, when are you going to finally make a video of me? I'm serious. We need to do this. I wanna be in porn, man!"

I see this anecdote hasn't strengthened my case any. How can I claim to be an "accidental pornographer" when I have all *the equipment?*

The first time Pro visited my studio, he thought out loud: "You actually have strobe lights."

And what *legitimate* business could I have residing in a Navy shipyard ghetto devoid of any diversions save for sailors and seedy bars? It may be possible to accept an author of global ultramarginal cult standing not opting for New York or Los Angeles. But it's rather more difficult to concede much leeway to a vegetarian nondriver who opts to dwell where the only restaurant within walking distance is McDonald's and still claims he's not there for "military meat."

Ah, but here's where my story gains some credibility, if only as a potential insanity defense: You see, I moved to this isolated Navy ghost town—where it rains even more than in neighboring Seattle—from San Diego, California, "military chaser" central, USA. And military porn video central.

And I fled to escape my apprenticeship in military beefcake photography.

*San Diego, California—January 1996:*
  *Pornographer's Apprentice*
Rewind five years.

I'm in the passenger seat of a cheap leased car, very slowly puttering through a mountainous stretch of San Diego County east toward the desert. Behind the wheel is a man of advanced years and failing health. His breath is rancid. He's subject to wild mood swings. He recites the same anecdotes and same old jokes with trying frequency, and rarely betrays the faintest interest in listening to anyone else. But for once, I've managed to catch and hold his attention, reading aloud to him from the *New Yorker.*

It's Susan Faludi's "The Money Shot," the part about the porn video former U.S. Marine John Wayne Bobbitt starred in to exhibit his surgically reattached penis.

David guffaws so loudly, is so delighted by the story, that I'm almost stoked. And mistakenly imagine that David might share my interest in Faludi's cultural commentary on how ejaculating onscreen in porn video has supplanted more traditional demonstrations of masculine prowess such as working in a shipyard. Only a discharge of David's intestinal gas prompts me to glance over and realize that he's no longer paying the slightest attention.

"I've decided to send her my galleys for *The Masculine Marine,*" I conclude. "I know it's a long shot. Probably we won't end up meeting over arugula and bottled water in L.A. But a blurb from Susan Faludi—"

David looks at me intently. He nods, indicating the landscape to our left. "I've often wondered," he intones, "how those rocks got there. "

Well, it's less of a non sequitur than it was twenty-four hours ago, when he made the same pronouncement at the same spot....

This is day two of my new part-time job, assisting David Lloyd on outdoor nude photo shoots of straight military men.

Yesterday the model was a brawny Coast Guardsman named Andy who chattered nervously the entire two hours it took us to reach the desert. On the ride there he was too polite—or scared—to comment on David's failure to observe the minimum speed limit and only once said, "Your turn signal's still on."

He did, however, put his foot down when David at last stopped the car and declared, "This is the place."

David's "ravine backdrop" was directly astride the highway and in clear view of its near-constant parade of retirees in RVs, who, confused by the fork in the road there, drove as slowly as David.

The Coast Guardsman balked.

I suggested, "Maybe just behind those rocks?"

David grimaced darkly. He raised his arms like a Joshua tree and bellowed, "There goes half the day right there!" We climbed fifty paces farther into the scrub.

At the conclusion of the shoot as we were packing up to leave Andy got some horrible cactus thing embedded in his foot and made a big deal of stoically yanking it out, for my benefit.

He was less stoic on the ride home, however, when David, in the thrall of another rambling stock narrative, momentarily mistook the treacherous two-lane mountain highway for Interstate 5 and drifted into the other lane. There were shouts, imprecations, and then apologies from Andy.

"Man! I'm sorry I grabbed the wheel. But you just missed hitting that car! We would have been dead! Man, you scared me!"

David graciously forgave him. Glancing at me in the rearview mirror, he rolled his eyes at this studly straight guy's nervous-nelly attack.

Today's model is a Marine. Because he's stationed north of San Diego at Camp Pendleton, he drives his own car to a rendezvous point on the edge of the desert.

Kris is of Scandinavian ancestry. He fits certain of my stereotypes of Marines and Scandinavians. Kris is so reserved that even David runs out of banter.

And when David pulls over to his ravine backdrop directly astride the highway, Kris evinces a European absence of inhibition. David hands him the girlie magazine and we simply stand there as Kris casually works up a hard-on. By the second roll Kris has clambered onto a high rock and in plain view of passing cars swings his enormous erection. Chortling, David produces a ruler and measures it. "By God!" he roars. "Eight and three-quarter inches! That's how big Mr. Smiley is!"

Pleased with the $500 he's just pocketed, Kris is slightly less taciturn on the ride back. Thinking of Susan Faludi, I ask him whether he sees any potential connection between having proven his masculinity in the Marine Corps and modeling.

"No. You can get into a lot of trouble doing this."

I realize I'm receiving instruction here: being rebellious and naughty is almost as much reward as money and attention.

As a third-generation Dutch American from suburban Grand Rapids, Michigan, with a Calvinist-cum-fundamentalist upbringing, I am not altogether dissimilar to Kris in terms of social restraint. This, I know, is a quality of mine that David values. To the extent I find the experience of witnessing more or less perfect physical specimens of the U.S. Armed Forces stripping and performing indecent acts sexually arousing, I don't betray it. Still, when David calls me up a few days later and reports that at the conclusion of a second shoot, this time in a studio, Swedish Marine Kris requested and was granted permission to ejaculate, I almost feel left out.

David had no choice but to reshoot Kris—hastily. All eight rolls of film he shot in the desert were overexposed beyond salvation.

Even on his best days, David has to shoot double or triple the number of images any other photographer would, owing to his shaky hands. Tremor is a common side effect of lithium, the medication David takes for his bipolar disorder.

David is puzzled as to why this should be so much more a problem outdoors than in the studio. When I ask him why he doesn't just use a faster shutter speed, he's at a loss to answer. It's never occurred to him to toy with the automatic settings on his Nikon, he confesses.

"I don't have time!"

David earns upward of $100,000 a year from his photography. His work has been published in virtually every gay skin magazine at home and abroad and is endlessly recycled in phone-sex ads and other second-use outlets. Who am I to tell him about f-stops?

"The shoot was a total loss!" he thunders, with such outrage and wonder you'd think he'd just witnessed a cloud of locusts descending on San Diego specifically intent on devouring his Agfachromes of the Swedish Marine's "Mr. Smiley." "But I still had to pay Kris the same money again. *In cash!*" In a quieter tone he thinks to add, "And of course you'll still get your check."

I know that when David does pay me it's as much for my company as anything. And he knows that I wouldn't help him sort through slides or type up correspondence for fifteen dollars an hour if I didn't enjoy hearing his stories.

And as outrageous as his demands sometimes are, I somehow still feel terribly guilty when I nervously announce to David that my roommate Alex Buchman is thinking of moving to Seattle.

He sees through me in an instant. "You are not seriously thinking of moving to Seattle!"

He looks more crestfallen than I anticipated. Given the one-sidedness of our exchanges, I don't like to think that David sees something of himself in me. It's easier to focus on his sighs about how hard it will be to find another assistant like me—someone he can carry on a conversation with *and* who "doesn't drool" over big-dicked Marines.

David grew up in Seattle. His final word is, "I give it two years, three at the most. You're not a Seattle kind of guy." Nodding with conviction he turns his head away and pronounces, "You'll be back."

### Bremerton, Washington—January 1999:
### Stiffed

Two years later *Military Trade* is almost off press. David is one of the "military chasers" interviewed. One of his naked Marines is on the cover.

But David suffers a massive stroke and dies some months before I write my English friend Mark Simpson that I've realized I'm not really a Seattle kind of guy. "Since I can't seem to face returning to San Diego, I think I might as well take advantage of being perhaps the only person in Seattle who can move to Bremerton without losing face."

Bremerton, Washington, is a downscale Pacific Northwest town located between the similarly depressed hometown of Kurt Cobain (Hoquiam/Aberdeen) and Seattle, with no Starbucks and only one employer, the U.S. Navy shipyard.

I'm drawn to an old brick apartment building of institutional appearance. Only after I move in do I learn that it was constructed during World War I as an annex to the Navy Yard Hotel.

The last time Bremerton flourished was World War II. Most of the storefronts are boarded up. But there are a lot of churches. And taverns.

Bremerton is notorious for its population of sexually aggressive women—"Fat chicks chasin' fellas in the Navy," in the offensive words of Seattle rapper Sir Mix-A-Lot's 1987 song "Bremelo."

I've never lived "on the wrong side of the tracks" before. By the end of my first week here I'm starting to feel a little creeped out. Walking through town I'm struck by the number of burned-out houses posted ARSON. REWARD. I pick up the local paper and read that a woman was raped in the parking lot below my bedroom window. A Friday evening crawl of waterfront bars leaves me struggling to picture myself fitting in here at all.

I'm about to give up for the night when I pass by a derelict tavern and notice that there are lights on inside. The door is open. I walk in and am immediately greeted, "Steve!" A gay submariner recognizes me from a book reading.

The Crow's Nest dates back a century. Knowing that Bremerton is too small and too working class to sustain a gay bar, the new owner aims for an unobtrusively gay-friendly mixed bar. Reopening night, the crowd is engagingly motley. There are more gay submariners, there are Bremelos—and on the barstool to my right there is a drunken bug-eyed misfit who announces that he is self-publishing a chapbook of poems about crossing Bremerton ferry.

"Steve writes about fairies too," remarks my submariner friend.

The DVD plays George Michael's "Outside" video. Just below the monitor, an old wooden placard reads:

WELCOME ABOARD.
THE LORD TAKES CARE OF DRUNKS AND SAILORS.

I find myself making eye contact with a sailor. When he goes to the men's room, I follow. But I don't get to stand next to him at the awkwardly intimate urinals—someone else beats me to it. Peeing next to the sailor is a thirtyish man sporting short hair and a golf cap. With aching clarity I overhear him inquire, "So...are you in the Navy?"

When the sailor leaves the bar, I somehow feel obliged to sidle up next to the luckless chaser.

He's startled, even shocked that I've pegged him. Buddy tells me that he doesn't like gay culture, he just likes guys. I mention an English writer friend who's edited a book called *Anti-Gay* and his invitation to take me to Plymouth.

"Oh. I've been to Plymouth. It's like Bremerton. I mean, it's a lot bigger. But," Buddy shakes his head, "they've got the same Bremelos."

I become a regular at the Crow's Nest. A sailor I meet there becomes something of a boyfriend. When he's out to sea, I hang out with Buddy. By summer we're drinking pals.

And what a summer it is. Weekend nights the bars are packed with sailors off the USS *Abraham Lincoln,* an aircraft carrier in town for a six-month overhaul. Buddy and I make a game of compiling weekly top-ten lists of our favorites. Even though—he is anxious that I understand this—he cannot himself be termed a military chaser. He's not a predator. "And," he reasons, "I also like firemen."

I don't disabuse Buddy of his conviction that he doesn't fit any stereotypes. And indeed, it seems that the only people who perceive Buddy as stereotypically gay are visiting urban gays.

I accompany Buddy on his nearly nightly rounds of the roughest dive bars on the waterfront. Buddy plays pool with sailors. I sit on bar stools and listen to career Navy alcoholics' sea stories.

These guys tend to come from small towns in the southern United States—or neighboring Idaho. Young men who never once jump on the ferry to Seattle by themselves, because they never have. Instead, they booze and brawl alongside the Bremelos.

Buddy takes to introducing me to local people as a "famous author"—a title that calls for too much explanation. One night I adjure my drinking pal, "Don't tell people I'm a famous author. Tell them I'm a famous photographer."

I'm half-joking. The only photos I've had published are in my own books. But among the thousands of *Lincoln* sailors, a half dozen or so who have become "downtown" regulars exude indisputable star quality, and one night it becomes more than I can bear.

We're in Buddy's favorite bar. I'm entertaining an out-of-town dignitary, a professor at one of the military academies. The prettiest of the *Lincoln* boys is there—drinking Bud by the pitcher, playing pool, and stealing the hearts or at least admiring glances from everyone present. He's winsome beyond measure, from his disarming constant grin to his tight Wrangler jeans to the heavily autographed cast on his broken arm. An inscription jumps out at me:

DON'T JERK OFF SO HARD

Buddy and the professor are merely charmed. And as for me....

When yet another young sailor staggers in, spots Castboy, and with unstudied passion immediately throws his arms tightly around him, I get all misty-eyed, struggle to recite Whitman, and drunkenly vow that I will not return to this bar without a camera because "That picture would have been worth more than all of my books put together."

Buddy is keen on the idea but cautions me that before I start taking any pictures of sailors in the bar a protocol must be devised. I should wait until the hour when everyone is a little drunk but not yet sloppy drunk. The first pictures must be of people we know—say, Buddy and a woman, and then with some other guy. And only then take pictures of a sailor, but still only with a girl.

"If anybody gives you trouble, I'll back you up."

There was trouble, all right. But not like Buddy expected.

The first night I worked up enough nerve to pop my electronic flash in a waterfront pool hall a sailor angrily confronted me: "Why are you taking pictures of him instead of me?"

Of course I obliged him. But this angered the sailor I had been taking pictures of. Losing the spotlight, he sulked. Seeing this, I reassured him, "Well, don't let it go to your head, but you definitely have the most potential as a model." That was Mike, the sailor with the cast on his arm.

When his best friend from the ship walked in, Mike proudly repeated my appraisal.

This sailor in turn took me aside and demanded, "Him? You're wasting your film. Dude! His ears are too big!" And that was Packard, the sailor who would end up starring in *Out of the Brig,* the porn video I made by accident.

### Bremerton, Washington—Summer 1999:
### Trouble Loves Me

As with any accident, memory blurs. This much is known:

That summer *Honcho* ran an interview with me to promote *Military Trade.* When I e-mailed the editor my thanks, I attached some JPGs of sailors drinking and playing pool. Doug McClemont wrote back that he liked the pictures. He invited me to shoot a few rolls of slide film for publication in his magazine.

At the time, I didn't own any strobe lights (much less any video equipment).

Of the three USS *Lincoln* sailors who'd fought over who was the most photogenic, one was in the brig and another was in a military treatment center for substance abuse. When I relayed *Honcho*'s invitation to Packard, he expressed skepticism. "Yeah, but how much would it pay?"

I told him how much.

Packard may or may not have dropped his pool stick. It seems like it was only a matter of hours before I'd shot enough rolls of Kodak EPP to FedEx to New York and woke up to a voice mail from Doug telling me the pictures were okay—only, "They're a little dark. If you can, try to get just a basic monolight."

For once, I wasn't "in between books." I had the money, but what motivated me to spend $1,000 on basic studio lighting equipment was not the promise of selling more layouts. I wanted to spare my models the shame of telltale amateur shadows.

That summer the (beefy but reclusive) Navy master-at-arms living next door to me vacated his one-room apartment. I toyed with the extravagant idea of renting the "studio," but not seriously—until the building manager accepted a rental application for the unit from a Bremelo with two small children.

"Well, I'll have the linoleum replaced for you." My landlady was perplexed but also impressed at my renting two apartments. "And about the cracks in the walls—"

She didn't argue when I told her I liked the room exactly as it was.

I had sense enough not to gush about how especially fond I was of the vintage Murphy bed and its stained mattress. Instead, I asked her what she knew about how the building had been furnished during World War II when it served as officers' quarters.

After I dragged up from the basement a battered chair and matching nightstand, my studio was ready. In the thirteen months I rented it I didn't change a detail.

That summer I was prescribed Paxil (paroxetene), an anti-depressant/anti-anxiety drug in the same family of selective serotinin reuptake inhibitors as Prozac. Overall, the medication made me more self-assured and confident. Bold, even. I would not have dived into neophysique photography without it.

Paxil also abated some of my anxieties about turning into David Lloyd.

But one side effect of Paxil resulted in a new and unwelcome physical resemblance to David. From my first video recording made in the new studio:

PACKARD: I can see why you like the "steady shot" feature so much.

ZEELAND: [mock confrontationally] So what are you trying to say?

PACKARD: I can see your hands shaking right now.

ZEELAND: [Remains silent]

PACKARD: [Coughs and looks away]

The camcorder was an impulse purchase, prompted by cues from sailors I spoke with about modeling. The most succinct and memorable:

"So...you only take *still* pictures?"

It was in answer to another magazine editor's invitation that I became acquainted with videomaker Dink Flamingo of ActiveDuty.com. At the close of my interview with him for *Unzipped* Dink confided that he'd never aspired to become a pornographer. His ambition had always been to be a journalist.

We agreed to "trade places for a day." Dink promised to contribute some authentic accounts of erotic liaisons with "barracks bad boys" to Alex Buchman's nonfiction anthology in progress. I pledged to try my hand at playing auteur in his scandal-ridden, sordid "adult amateur video" subgenre.

After patiently bearing with me for nine long months, Dink breathed satisfaction and relief upon receipt of the labor of love I finally delivered.

My timing, however, could not have been worse. The scheduled release date for my video celebrating real-life military deserters coincided with the bombings of the World Trade Center and the Pentagon.

Still, my three masturbating sailors cannot really be accused of "disgracing the military." The title *Out of the Brig* is no fantasy; it's documentary. The sailors in it are real-life tattooed Navy "bad boys" who really have broken the rules, have done their time, and are no longer on active duty—are no longer answerable to anyone. (Even if at the scheduled release date one of them had not yet turned himself in. Had Congress officially declared war, and had he been arrested, he could have faced the firing squad.)

**Barracks Bad Boys:**
*The Movie*

The style of my directorial debut is a cross between early Dirk Yates and early Andy Warhol. With, I'd like to think, a human face.

But not mine.

FIRST SAILOR: Approximately three minutes into the opening sequence, which stars Packard, you can hear me say: "You know, you could even sort of self-direct this" (as I hand him a second remote, and flip over the camcorder viewfinder so that he can zoom in and out to...self-direct).

SECOND SAILOR: After a short introductory scene (unscripted and shot in one take at a retro adult video arcade just outside the shipyard), I don't do much "directing." This one stars

Pro. He masturbates watching DVDs on my living room TV.

THIRD SAILOR: The first two sequences are exactly twenty minutes long. The closing sequence is a film within a film, and a full hour long. It's an essay by itself, too. For my purpose here, it's enough to tell you that I miscalculated in thinking that for this shoot I had an assistant who would effectively play "Steve" to my "David." But when the door to my own studio slammed shut with me locked out, I was surprised but not altogether displeased.

And when an hour and a half later I was allowed back in the room and rewound through some of the tape, I knew that this was it. My "sailors gone bad" had given me enough "raw footage" to meet the basic requirements of the amateur military porn video idiom. Now I could give myself over to endless hours lovingly *editing*.

### *Bremerton, Washington—January 2003*

By the time you read this I will no longer be in Bremerton, Washington. Every last one of the active-duty sailors I photographed has long since departed. Two or three of them transferred to distant duty stations; two or three received honorable discharges. Between twenty and thirty were kicked out of the Navy for "unauthorized absence" and/or drug use. In February 2002, the Navy announced that all of the ships currently home-ported in Bremerton would be moved elsewhere. Also, that the block of 100-year-old buildings adjacent to the Navy shipyard—including the historic Crow's Nest tavern—would be demolished to provide a "security buffer" against terrorist attack. But the bar shut down even before the wrecking ball hit, after the thirty-seven-year-old owner was found dead under mysterious circumstances.

Pro has long since moved back to Texas. But he's kept in

touch. And at one point when I was too long in replying to his e-mail he left me a voice mail:

"Steve! Come out of your fucking Pax-hole!"

Actually, I'd quit Paxil and sworn off maintenance drugs of any sort just before September 11, 2001.

"Are we still friends or what? Dude! *I shot my seed on your TV!*"

It isn't very often I turn on my TV, and almost never when I'm alone. But one special occasion was the day I opened a package from Dink Flamingo, stretched out on the couch, hit the remote, and watched *Out of the Brig.*

And noticed I had missed a spot when I cleaned the monitor.

# ABOUT THE AUTHORS

**SHANE ALLISON** is the editor of *Hot Cops, Backdraft, College Boys, Homo Thugs, Hard Working Men,* and *Black Fire.* His stories have graced the pages of several Cleis Press anthologies, including four lustful editions of *Best Gay Erotica.* His first book of poems, *Slut Machine,* is out from Rebel Satori Press.

**RALOWE TRINITROTOLUENE AMPU** (ralowesconfused-suburbanlaughter.com) is an annoying black homosexual asshole living in San Francisco. When not cruising bathrooms at chain department stores and on college campuses, or watching porn, she raps, kind of, and was an instigator, back when, of Gay Shame.

**DRUB** (drubskin.com), an illustrator of erotica for more than fifteen years, has displayed in galleries in Europe and North America and published in *Gay Amsterdam News, Blue, Freshmen* and *S.M.U.T.*; his art has promoted the 2006 Seattle

Erotic Art Festival, the Tom of Finland Art Festival and Folsom Street Fair '07.

**TIM DOODY** (timdoody.me) has had work published in various journals, among them *Brevity, The Brooklyn Rail,* and *Word Riot.* ABC-TV's "Nightline" included Doody in a national list of "particularly troublesome, even dangerous, anarchists," and Rush Limbaugh made fun of him and his last name on the air.

**TREBOR HEALEY** (treborhealey.com) is the author of the Ferro-Grumley and Violet Quill Award–winning novel, *Through It Came Bright Colors,* as well as a collection of poems, *Sweet Son of Pan,* and a short-story collection, *A Perfect Scar & Other Stories.* He lives in Los Angeles.

**ARDEN HILL** is an all around queer who bends genera and gender. Hir erotica has been published in *Best Gay Erotica 2008, Boys in Heat,* and loveyoudivine.com. In the fall ze will begin a PhD program for English and Creative writing at The University of Nebraska at Lincoln.

**LEE HOUCK** (grammarpiano.com) was born in Chattanooga, Tennessee and now lives in Queens, New York. His first novel, *Yield,* was published by Kensington in 2010. His writing appears in several anthologies and in two limited-edition chapbooks, *Collection* (2006) and *Warnings* (2009.) He is at work on a new novel.

**DALE LAZAROV** (dalelazarov.tumblr.com) is the writer/editor of gay erotic comics such as *STICKY* (drawn by Steve MacIsaac), *MANLY* (drawn by Amy Colburn) and *NIGHTLIFE* (drawn by Bastian Jonsson), all published by Bruno Gmünder Verlag. He's collaborating on several new gay erotic comics projects and lives in Chicago.

**DAVID MAY** contributed to *Drummer* and other gay skin magazines in the 1980s, published two classic story collections in the 1990s (including *Madrugada: A Cycle of Erotic Fictions*, reprinted in 2009 by Nazca Plains), and his work has appeared in many anthologies. He lives in Seattle.

**ANDREW MCCARTHY** (notshadyjustfierce.com) is a New York City multidisciplinary artist. He cofounded, designed, and wrote for a number of defunct gay publications, including *Glamma* and *Clikque*. His work can be found in *Best Gay Erotica 2008*, *Sticker Shock* and *Reproduce & Revolt*.

**ROBERT PATRICK** makes a meager living reviewing gay male adult movies, and though he would rather *make* gay male movies or at least gay males, he is happier than he was writing and directing a thousand stage productions from Anchorage to Capetown, and he was pretty damn near blissful then.

**SIMON SHEPPARD** (simonsheppard.com) is making his seventeenth appearance in the *Best Gay Erotica* series. He edited the Lambda Award–winning *Homosex: Sixty Years of Gay Erotica* and *Leathermen* and wrote *In Deep: Erotic Stories; Kinkorama; Sex Parties 101,* and *Hotter Than Hell.* His work has appeared in nearly three hundred anthologies.

**CHARLIE VÁZQUEZ** (firekingpress.com) is a *criollo* warrior of Cuban and Puerto Rican descent. His work has appeared in several print and online publications, and he hosts a reading series in New York that features queer fiction and poetry. His second novel, *Contraband*, was published by Rebel Satori Press in 2010.

**ALANA NOËL VOTH**'s stories have appeared in *Boy Crazy*, *Oysters & Chocolate*, *Best Women's Erotica 2009*, and *Best Gay Erotica 2008*. One of her prized possessions is a first edition copy of *Naked Lunch*. She loves spicy tuna rolls and red wine, and is working on a novel.

**THOM WOLF** (myspace.com/thomwolfspace) has published two erotic novels, *Words Made Flesh* and *The Chain*, and collaborated with Kevin Killian on "Too Far" for *Frozen Tear II*, funded by the Arts Council of England. He lives with husband Liam in northeast England, where he studies creative writing and dabbles in gay porn.

**STEVEN ZEELAND** (stevenzeeland.com) is the preeminent chronicler of homoeroticism in the U.S. military. His books include *Barrack Buddies and Soldier Lovers*, *Sailors and Sexual Identity*, *The Masculine Marine*, *Military Trade*, and the forthcoming photo collection *SEADOG: Navy Town Nightlife*. He lives in Bremerton, Washington.

# ABOUT THE EDITOR

**RICHARD LABONTE** (tattyhill@gmail.com) was a gay book-seller for twenty years, has written book reviews for more than thirty years, has edited about thirty (mostly erotic) gay antholo-gies for Cleis Press and Arsenal Pulp Press, and spends his week-ends as a kitchen assistant preparing lunches and dinners for as many as sixty people. He lives on beautiful Bowen Island, a short ferry ride from Vancouver, with husband Asa Dean Liles and their two dogs, both (the dogs, not the men) frustrated because they have not yet caught one of the island's hundreds of free-roaming deer, which would be a natural thing to do, but so very wrong. Several editions of the *Best Gay Erotica* series, which he has edited since 1996, have been Lambda Literary Award finalists, and two have won, as has *First Person Queer* (Arsenal Pulp), coedited with Lawrence Schimel.

# More Gay Erotic Stories from Richard Labonté

**Muscle Men**
*Rock Hard Gay Erotica*
Edited by Richard Labonté

*Muscle Men* is a celebration of the body beautiful, where men who look like Greek gods are worshipped for their outsized attributes. Editor Richard Labonté takes us into the erotic world of body builders and the men who desire them.
ISBN 978-1-57344-392-0 $14.95

---

**Bears**
*Gay Erotic Stories*
Edited by Richard Labonté

These uninhibited symbols of blue-collar butchness put all their larger-than-life attributes—hairy flesh, big bodies, and that other party-size accoutrement—to work in these close encounters of the furry kind.
ISBN 978-1-57344-321-0 $14.95

**Country Boys**
*Wild Gay Erotica*
Edited by Richard Labonté

Whether yielding to the rugged charms of that hunky ranger or skipping the farmer's daughter in favor of his accommodating son, the men of *Country Boys* unabashedly explore sizzling sex far from the city lights.
ISBN 978-1-57344-268-8 $14.95

**Daddies**
*Gay Erotic Stories*
Edited by Richard Labonté

Silver foxes. Men of a certain age. Guys with baritone voices who speak with the confidence that only maturity imparts. The characters in *Daddies* take you deep into the world of father figures and their admirers.
ISBN 978-1-57344-346-3 $14.95

**Boy Crazy**
*Coming Out Erotica*
Edited by Richard Labonté

From the never-been-kissed to the most popular twink in town, *Boy Crazy* is studded with explicit stories of red-hot hunks having steamy sex.
ISBN 978-1-57344-351-7 $14.95

# Get Under the Covers
# With These Hunks

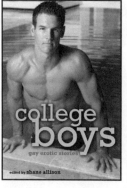

# Get Under the Covers
# With These Hunks

**Hot Cops**
*Gay Erotic Stories*
Edited by Shane Allison

"From smooth and fit to big and hairy…it's like a downtown locker room where everyone has some sort of badge."—*Bay Area Reporter*
ISBN 978-1-57344-277-0   $14.95

---

**Special Forces**
*Gay Military Erotica*
Edited by Phillip Mackenzie, Jr.

*Special Forces* pays homage to the heroic hunks on the frontlines who are always willing to protect and serve their fellow men.
ISBN 978-1-57344-372-2   $14.95

**Leathermen**
*Gay Erotic Stories*
Edited by Simon Sheppard

Offering unforgettably explicit stories of edge play at its most arousing, this collection of one-fisted reading explores the depths of fear and desire among leathermen.
ISBN 978-1-57344-322-7   $14.95

**Backdraft**
*Fireman Erotica*
Edited by Shane Allison

"Seriously: This book is so scorching hot that you should box it with a fire extinguisher and ointment. It will burn more than your fingers." —*Tucson Weekly*
ISBN 978-1-57344-325-8   $14.95

**Hard Hats**
*Gay Erotic Stories*
Edited by Neil Plakcy

With their natural brand of macho and the sheen of honest sweat on flesh, men with tool belts rank among the hottest icons in gay erotic fantasy.
ISBN 978-1-57344-312-8   $14.95

---

# The Bestselling Novels of James Lear

## The Mitch Mitchell Mystery Series

### The Back Passage
By James Lear

"Lear's lusty homage to the classic whodunit format (sorry, Agatha) is wonderfully witty, mordantly mysterious, and enthusiastically, unabashedly erotic!"
—Richard Labonté, Book Marks, Q Syndicate
ISBN 978-1-57344-243-5 $13.95

### The Secret Tunnel
By James Lear

"Lear's prose is vibrant and colourful... This isn't porn accompanied by a wah-wah guitar, this is porn to the strains of Beethoven's *Ode to Joy*, each vividly realised ejaculation accompanied by a fanfare and the crashing of cymbals."
—*Time Out London*
ISBN 978-1-57344-329-6 $13.95

### A Sticky End
*A Mitch Mitchell Mystery*
By James Lear

To absolve his best friend and sometimes lover from murder charges, Mitch races around London finding clues while bedding the many men eager to lend a hand—or more.
ISBN 978-1-57344-395-1 $14.95

### The Low Road
By James Lear

Author James Lear expertly interweaves spies and counterspies, scheming servants and sadistic captains, tavern trysts and prison orgies into this delightfully erotic work.
ISBN 978-1-57344-364-7 $14.95

### Hot Valley
By James Lear

"Lear's depiction of sweaty orgies... trumps his Southern war plot, making the violent history a mere inconsequential backdrop to all of Jack and Aaron's sticky mischief. Nice job."
—*Bay Area Reporter*
ISBN 978-1-57344-279-4 $14.95

Ordering is easy! Call us toll free or fax us to place your MC/VISA order.
You can also mail the order form below with payment to:
Cleis Press, 2246 Sixth St., Berkeley, CA 94710.

## ORDER FORM

| QTY | TITLE | PRICE |
|-----|-------|-------|
| | | |
| | | |
| | | |
| | | |
| | | |
| | | |
| | | |
| | | |

| | | |
|--|--|--|
| | SUBTOTAL | |
| | SHIPPING | |
| | SALES TAX | |
| | TOTAL | |

Add $3.95 postage/handling for the first book ordered and $1.00 for each additional book. Outside North America, please contact us for shipping rates. California residents add 9.75% sales tax. Payment in U.S. dollars only.

**\* Free book of equal or lesser value. Shipping and applicable sales tax extra.**

**Cleis Press • Phone: (800) 780-2279 • Fax: 510-845-8001**
**orders@cleispress.com • www.cleispress.com**
**You'll find more great books on our website**

**Follow us on Twitter @cleispress • Friend/fan us on Facebook**